MW01256844

The Kudzu That Ate Yazoo City

William L. Jenkins

xulon PRESS

The Kudzu That Ate Yazoo City
By William L. Jenkins
kudzu@cox.net

Printed in the United States of America

ISBN 1-594678-01-4

www.xulonpress.com

Bless y'all
William Jenkins

Dedication

This book is dedicated to my family,
Pop
Mother
Ellen
Linda
Norman
Marietta
Tommy
and Louis

"If I can make people smile,
then I have served my purpose for God."
Red Skelton

Table of Contents

"History will be kind to me for I intend to write it"
Winston Churchill (1874-1965)

Preface

"It is easier for a camel to go through the eye of a needle than for a rich man to enter the kingdom of God."
(Mark 10:25)

Thank God I wasn't cursed with wealth. I didn't even come close! Growing up poor in rural Mississippi in the 1950s was enriching in ways that matter. That experience formed the basis for appreciating the many blessings, gifts, and opportunities that life brought to my doorstep. This book recounts some of those nostalgic, youthful memories, tinged with the patina of age and perspective, and the embellishments of my recollections.

This is a book that should be taken lightly. It is an unabashed mixture of true memories, half-true stories and outright figments of my imagination.

Any resemblance to persons, living or dead, is more than coincidental. Everything written within this text is meant to be an expression of love and appreciation for all the wonderful people of Yazoo City, and especially those who lived on Graball Hill, who influenced my childhood. There is an expression, "it takes a village" to raise a child, but I know it took a (Yazoo) City to help form its youth into the adults we have become.

Writing this book makes me concerned about the scripture, "*But I tell you that men will have to give account on the day of judgment for every careless word they have spoken.*" (Matthew 12:36)

There are more stories where these came from. There may be a "Kudzu II" about you!

Acknowledgements

Behind every successful man there is a woman — pointing out his mistakes and kicking his behind over the finish line. First and foremost, I wish to acknowledge the help of my wife, Anita, in prompting me to finish this book. She heard me talk about it for over a decade. Her insights, suggestions, corrections, and master proof reading skills made it a much better effort than it would otherwise have been.

I want to especially thank my sister Linda for collecting data that assisted my sketchy memory of particular events.

I want to thank my family, and the cast of characters, living and deceased, who played a role in my life and in the pages of this book. Thank you, especially, my friends for offering your encouragement to complete this long promised book.

Introduction

KUDZU *(kud' zoo)*

Description: Kudzu is a climbing, semi-woody, perennial vine in the pea family. Deciduous leaves are alternate and compound, with three broad leaflets up to 4 inches across. Leaflets may be entire or deeply 2-3 lobed with hairy margins. Individual flowers, about 1/2 inch long, are purple, highly fragrant and borne in long hanging clusters. Flowering occurs in late summer and is soon followed by production of brown, hairy, flattened, seed pods, each of which contains three to ten hard seeds.

Ecological Threat: Kudzu kills or degrades other plants by smothering them under a solid blanket of leaves, by girdling woody stems and tree trunks, and by breaking branches or uprooting entire trees and shrubs through the sheer force of its weight. Once established, Kudzu plants grow rapidly, extending as much as 60 feet per season at a rate of about one foot per day. This vigorous vine may extend 32-100 feet in length, with stems 1/2 - 4 inches in diameter. Kudzu roots are fleshy, with massive tap roots 7 inches or more in diameter, 6 feet or more in length, and weighing as much as 400 pounds. As many as thirty vines may grow from a single root crown.

YAZOO CITY, MISSISSIPPI

Yazoo City, MS (Population 2000: 14,500) is located forty miles northwest of Jackson, the state capital, on the Yazoo River, at the edge of the Mississippi Delta. Named for the extinct Yazoo Native American (Indian) tribe, Yazoo City is the county seat for Yazoo County, the state's largest (920 square miles). The Yazoo River begins at the confluence of the Tallahatchie and Yalobusha Rivers, and flows 188 miles into the Mississippi River at Vicksburg. Yazoo is an Indian word for "river of death," perhaps a reference to the muddy river.

CHAPTER 1

And Then There Was Kudzu

"Life's a voyage that's homeward bound."
Herman Melville (1819-1891)

"A farmer went out to sow his seed. As he was scattering the seed, some fell along the path; it was trampled on, and the birds of the air ate it up. Some fell on rock, and when it came up, the plants withered because they had no moisture. Other seed fell among thorns, which grew up with it and choked the plants. Still other seed fell on good soil. It came up and yielded a crop, a hundred times more than was sown." When he said this, he called out, "He who has ears to hear, let him hear." (Luke 8:5-8)

The Rev. Mr. Goodbody used this text many times when I was a boy attending worship at the Assured Brethren Church in my hometown of Yazoo City, Mississippi. I wasn't positive the original Greek manuscripts on this text actually spoke about kudzu, but everyone in Yazoo City believed it was true. We knew the "choking plant" all too well. Kudzu had choked our farms, our barns, and most of the city. Later in my studies at seminary, I researched extensively the Hebrew texts and found there was no mention of kudzu in the Garden of Eden. No surprise there. Then, one day I found it: "kud-zoo". There it was, right in the Greek text. It was biblical. Even Jesus was annoyed with the useless green vine. I often wondered why God created such things as snakes and kudzu. They serve no visible useful purpose. They do, however, offer a good metaphor for evil, and Jesus seized the moment. He, who has ears to hear, let him hear.

Kudzu, for the benefit of the uninitiated, is a vine. It looks like ivy, but looks can be deceiving. Kudzu is a fast growing parasitic weed, which quickly covers everything in its path; trees, houses, roads, abandoned cars, yards, barns, you name it! I remember the night the Calhoun family, who lived just over the crest of Graball Hill, left Poochie, their lazy, black and tan hound, sleeping on the back porch. In the morning, kudzu had overtaken the back yard and porch. Poochie was never seen again. Coincidence? I think not.

Growing kudzu is not difficult, but it is an adventure that will change your life. The stuff grows anywhere, even on asphalt. It's a vine with attitude. You plant kudzu by throwing a little piece on the ground, then running as fast as you can to get out of its way. For heaven's sake, do not fertilize it. However, we found high detergent 10W30 motor oil cuts down on the static sparks kudzu creates as it races across metal objects, such as cars set up on blocks in the front yard. The real challenge was keeping it out of the vegetable gardens. Kudzu doesn't understand crop rotation; once it sets in, there are no other crops. Even the pigs refused to eat it. If you have pesky neighbors, plant it along the property line, and they will soon disappear. No, I literally mean disappear. You can plant the stuff anytime, but I recommend doing it at night, so the neighbors cannot take photos that can and will be used in a court of law. And don't waste time trying herbicides to control it. That only makes kudzu mad, and the last thing you want growing on your property is angry kudzu. You may want to consider selling your house, but expect to take a hit on the selling price when the appraiser checks the "kudzu" box.

Legend has it that kudzu was imported from Japan in 1876 when it was displayed at the Philadelphia Centennial Celebration. Might have known the Yankees were involved in it someway. Agriculturalists were amazed at the plant's rapid growth. At first, it was seen as a remedy for soil erosion, or as food for cows. But as we learned too late, cows may chew the cud, but cows do not chew the kudzu. It was a classic case of a good idea gone wrong. I don't know if kudzu ever stopped soil erosion. Once it starts growing, you never see the soil underneath it again, so who can tell for sure? You might say kudzu got away from the agriculturalists, but to use kudzu and "got away" in the same sentence would be redundant. Goats may eat it, but not nearly fast enough. Whatever natural enemy it may have had in Japan, kudzu found an extremely hospitable environment in the hot, humid South, especially around Yazoo City. Guess that's where Mississippi got its "Hospitality State" nickname. The rich delta soil only encouraged it. The kudzu vines eventually covered millions of acres throughout the South, swallowing everything in its path, including all of Graball Hill and a large portion of Yazoo City, my hometown. "King Kudzu" became a serious threat to "King Cotton," the prime crop Mississippi grew for over a century. And then, the Depression came.

The 1940s have been called the heyday of kudzu. After the Civilian Conservation Corp planted 80 million kudzu crowns, many people continued to "sing the praises" of the persistent perennial. Literally. For example, a barbershop quartet, The Kudzu Krooners, became quite popular. Their biggest hit was, "I'll Grow on You." Years later, the Coasters changed the lyrics to "Poison Ivy" (a more popular plant) and made a mint.

In Botany 101 at Holmes Junior College, I learned that kudzu is a legume, and a kissing cousin to the black-eyed pea. I must confess the thought of kudzu kissing is particularly distasteful. Once established, it produces a vine that is almost as hard as wood when the plant pretends to die in winter. Catfish Calhoun started an enterprising lawn mowing business where he mowed several lawns each week. Then, it dawned on him, why not have a kudzu clipping service? Rather than once a week, which was fine for the grass, he could clip the kudzu every day. Rumor has it he was Yazoo City's first millionaire; at least he was one of the few people who turned kudzu into cash.

My brother, Tommy, and I thought we found a commercial use for kudzu when we used the dried vines as a substitute for cigarettes. We couldn't afford real cigarettes, and even if we could, Yazoo City was so small that Mr. Wiggins at the Graball Kwik Stop and Bait Shop, would tell our mother, and she would set our "butts" on fire. Not only did the kudzu smoke make us sicker than Sister Meeks' cow, it made me give up the idea of ever smoking anything again.

A recent study at my alma mater, Delta State University, home of the "Fighting Okra", and whose alternative mascot is the "Kamikaze Kudzu", showed kudzu reduced alcoholism among rats. No one bothered to mention it was kudzu that drove the rats to drink in the first place.

On a recent trip home, my sister Linda gave me some kudzu jelly to go on my breakfast toast. It was made from the kudzu blossom, and to be honest, was quite good. But then, when have you ever had bad jelly? Hope springs eternal that someday, someone will find a use for kudzu.

Alas, we Southerners have accepted that kudzu has

"taken root", and has become a permanent part of our culture and environment. A few futile optimists still hope for the good old days when you didn't need to worry about losing your car to the wicked weed while doing your weekly grocery shopping at the Piggly Wiggly. Most of us have accepted the inevitable, and are learning to live with it. Some even write verse about kudzu.

> "*Ah, you may have watched the black snake run*
> *To the shaded hole from the blistering sun*
> *And you may have seen the swallow's flight*
> *And the shooting star in the deep dark night:*
> *But until you have watched the Kudzu grow*
> *You have never seen the fastest show.*"

Ollie Reeves, *Time Magazine*, 1944.

Amen, Ollie!

CHAPTER 2

Mingo Chito and the Yazoo Nation

"The universal brotherhood of man is our most precious possession."
Mark Twain (1835-1910)

This would be a great name for a rock band. However, Mingo Chito (MING-oh CHEE-toe) is the name the Yazoo Nation of Native Americans (Indians) gave to their "Chief Big", or as we would say, Big Chief. Yazoo City High School named its student yearbook in honor of this legendary tribal leader.

It is not politically correct these days to call Native Americans "Indians". I assure you, when our high school named its mascot the Indians we meant no disrespect. We envisioned the mighty Yazoo warriors, who struck fear in the hearts of their rivals, as indeed our football team did every Friday night in the fall upon the gridiron battlefield. We played against teams with relatively docile names, such as the Vicksburg Greenies. The Yazoo Indians were a people of courage and honor.

San Diego State University's mascot is the Aztec, another extinct Native American nation with a rich legacy. A group of students showed up one day at SDSU, saying they were Aztec descendants. I was thrilled, because it was like Jurassic Park, where extinct beings came back to life. The "reincarnated" Aztecs said they were offended by the SDSU mascot. So the school launched an extensive venture to come up with a less offensive name. I like to be helpful, so I nominated the avocado, a green fruit (or is it a vegetable?) grown in the San Diego area as the new SDSU mascot. That wouldn't offend anyone, I thought. After all, my alma mater, Delta State University, selected okra as our mascot. How cool is that? SDSU put the matter up for a vote among the faculty, students and alumni. The final vote: Keep the Aztecs (35,146), Abstain (7), Avocados (1). The seven abstentions were the magnificent seven Aztec descendants, and we all know who voted for the Avocado. After suffering this landslide loss, I accepted the reality that the Aztecs and Yazoos are great mascots after all, because the noble tribes live on in honor at SDSU and Yazoo City High School.

Hundreds of years ago, the Yazoo Indians settled the area that now bears their name. The tribe, now extinct, was never large. They were a brave, fierce, and warlike people, who always fought to the death. Maybe that's why they are extinct! Some early settlers said that in the Indian vernacular Yazoo meant death. One legend has it that when the Yazoos arrived in the Delta, they found a race of giant people whom they conquered. Centuries later, the Choctaws and Chickasaws moved into the area, and subdued and befriended the Yazoos. We will never know for sure the riches of the legends that disappeared with the Yazoos.

I once heard that Native Americans did not understand the white man's concept of owning land. How does one own land? We may hold a deed, but ultimately, we are temporary trustees, and the land will pass on to someone else's stewardship sooner or later. That is why a handful of cloth and beads worth $24.00 for Manhattan Island looked like a good deal to the Lenape Indians in 1626.

Manifest Destiny is the story of the white man's acquisition of land once occupied by American Indians. The Yazoo Nation would not escape destiny. Among the first European explorers to the region now known as the Yazoo-Mississippi Delta was Hernando DeSoto in 1540. DeSoto received credit for discovering the Mississippi River, but I'm sure the Yazoos knew about the Mississippi long before Hernando arrived. The French explorer, La Salle, named the Yazoo River in 1682.

Yazoo holds the dubious distinction of an early scandal in American history, and my hometown was completely innocent. No sooner had the new nation been formed, when in 1795, some individuals in the state of Georgia formed the Yazoo Land Company. From what I understand, Georgia claimed all the land to its west, including present day states of Alabama and Mississippi. They referred to the vast area as Yazoo County, Georgia. It was a land scam, and the "Yazoo Land Bubble" burst. This ended the first attempt to settle the Indian lands.

Yazoo County was formed in 1823. In 1820, the Choctaws ceded their land in the Treaty of Doak's Stand, and moved west as part of the migration some call "The Trail of Tears". Many Choctaws remained in Mississippi, but most left for Oklahoma, and points west. Settlers quickly moved into the former Indian lands. Yazoo City, where the hills, Delta, and river converge, was a logical place for a settlement. Although several surrounding counties were carved from it, Yazoo is still Mississippi's largest county, with 920 square miles, but far from the most populous.

Yazoo City was originally named Manchester. Plotted in the 1830s on acreage owned by Greenwood Leflore, a half

French, half Choctaw Indian planter, the town enjoyed its strategic location on the banks of the Yazoo River. Leflore County and its county seat, Greenwood, were named for this famous Mississippi native.

The Choctaws and Yazoos erected Indian mounds. Some mounds were three to four hundred feet in diameter. One was located at the foot of Broadway Hill. Inside these mounds were tomahawks, bowls and other Indian artifacts. They found grave vaults similar to modern ones, only larger, ten or twelve feet long. That is why we believe the early Indians were giants. Since no bones were in the vaults, we may assume the giants practiced cremation.

No doubt, the Yazoo Indians found Graball Hill a perfect place for their village. From Graball Hill, one may see for miles over the flat Delta. One could imagine that the Yazoos invited their Choctaws, Chickasaws and Natchez neighbors to Yazoo Village for a cricket match. I visualize the Natchez tribe's sad trek home down the Natchez Trace as they returned home from the tournament, where they came in third behind the Yazoos and Choctaws.

Imagination can be a wonderful thing. Because of our poverty, and in the days before television and movie special effects, we allowed our imagination to take us places we could never travel. As a lad, I remember thinking how nice it was that we lived right next to what must have been sacred ground for the Yazoo Nation. Their youngsters romped over the same hillside and fields where my siblings, Ellen, Linda, Norman, Marietta, Tommy, Louis and I played. Maybe they fished in the Old North Pond. Maybe they planted corn in the same field where we did. Maybe the three giant pecan trees that stood between our house and the highway provided the Yazoos with delicious provisions. Sometimes, when Topey, the Righteous Wonder Dog, and I played alone, I imagined finding a Yazoo Indian lad hiding in the kudzu; my imaginary friend who would teach me ancient things white men never knew. I named him Little Mingo, the son of the chief, who was destined to grow up and become a great leader of the mighty Yazoo Nation. We became blood brothers, and although we spoke different languages, we shared many boyhood discoveries on Graball Hill.

Like their cousins, the Mohicans, the Yazoos gave up more than their land. An estimated 1700 Yazoos made up the Yazoo Nation at its peak in the 1700s. No doubt, many of the Yazoos died fighting other Native Americans, as I am sure they did for hundreds of years. The tribe, probably a branch of the Choctaws, was closely aligned with the Natchez Indians, and suffered near annihilation in retaliation for the Fort Rosalie massacre at Natchez in 1729. Only a handful of Yazoo Indians survived into the early 1800s, and those eventually vanished.

I remember finding Yazoo arrowheads on Graball Hill. We took those arrowheads for granted back then. I can even tell you exactly where you most likely will find some more still today, but the family that now lives there would not like it if folks started digging up their back yard. I wish I still had one, to carry my imagination back to Graball Hill, Little Mingo, and the Yazoo Nation.

On second thought, maybe we should leave them buried under the kudzu; sacred relics of a brave and noble people.

CHAPTER 3

Yazoo City, Kudzu Capital

"One must be poor to know the luxury of living."
Guillaume de Salluste Du Bartas

There really is a place called Yazoo City, Mississippi. But please learn how to say it correctly. It's YAZZ'-oo. Not YOZZ'-oo. Think JAZZ, and replace the J with a Y. YAZZ-oo. My sister Linda, on one of her trips, ran into a woman who asked her, "Where are you from?" "Yazoo City, Mississippi," Linda said. The lady laughed, "That's the funniest name I ever heard for a town." "Where are you from?" Linda asked politely. "Oh, I am from Pocatello, Idaho," she said, not seeing the irony in her reply.

I'll be the first to admit, Mississippi has some unusual names; Biloxi, Tchula, Belzoni, Hot Coffee, Tallahatchie, and Tishomingo, just to name a few. The early Methodist circuit riders in North Mississippi had a circuit named "Yellow Butcher" until they discovered it was actually a Native American word, Yalobusha. Many names reflect their Choctaw and Chickasaw origins, including Yazoo.

During the Civil War, Yazoo City was home to a

Confederate shipyard located at the top of Broadway Hill. The shipbuilders rolled the finished boats down Broadway on logs until they reached the banks of the Yazoo, where the ships were commissioned. When I was a boy, I remember seeing smoke coming from what appeared to be an abandoned lumberyard atop Broadway. Legend had it that it was a sawdust fire from the old shipyard still smoldering almost 100 years after the Yankees torched the shipyard.

The small community of Vaughan on the eastern edge of Yazoo County is where the famous railroad engineer, Casey Jones, died in the crash of his locomotive, the Cannonball Express in 1900.

In 1904, almost the entire town was destroyed in a fire some say is second only to the Great Chicago Fire, caused by Mrs. O'Leary's cow, in folklore. A woman, whom many believed to be a witch and a murderer, died in 1884. She vowed to come back from the grave in twenty years to burn down the town. The superstitious townsfolk placed a huge chain around her grave. Exactly twenty years after her death, Yazoo City almost burned to the ground. A few folks remembered the old woman's threat, and rushed to Glenwood Cemetery to find the links on the chain were broken. As a boy, I would often go to the Yazoo Witch's grave, and the broken chain was still there. The late Willie Morris told the story much better than I ever could, although I can still feel the chill of being close to evil.

The Great Mississippi River Flood of 1927 was the most destructive flood in American history, covering 27,000 square miles to a depth of up to 30 feet, causing $400 million in damage and killing 250 people.

In some strange way, the Great Depression was not as bad in Mississippi as elsewhere. Let me clarify. When you are dirt poor, being a little poorer is hardly noticeable. I could never tell the difference between 20 degrees below zero and 60 degrees below zero when I lived briefly in

Green Bay as a young adult. Cold is cold, and poor is poor. At least the folks in Yazoo City didn't starve, because they could grow crops in the fertile Delta soil.

The town had about 5,000 people or so in 1930, but grew much larger after Owen Cooper founded Mississippi Chemical Corporation in 1948. Following the war, the nation experienced its biggest baby boom. The soldiers returned, married their sweethearts, and the stork began making deliveries. I was one of those bundles delivered on the hottest and longest day of June in 1948. My father was too old to serve in WWII, and with only one eye, would not have qualified if he was younger. However, he didn't want to miss out on the baby boom, so he and mother regularly contributed to Yazoo City's population explosion. There were about 10,000 residents in the 1950s and 1960s, making the town large enough to offer some amenities, but small enough so that almost everyone knew each other.

Yazoo City is a lovely place, and was an almost ideal place to grow up in the 1950s, a place much like the fictional Mayberry, North Carolina; but even better, because Yazoo City was real. Crime was almost unknown. No one locked his or her front door. People visited each other, and took care of each other. There were successful farmers who lived in and around Yazoo City. Their capital was a boost to Yazoo City's post-war economy. In addition to an excellent school system, we had our own hospital, two banks, three movie houses and a drive in theater, a weekly newspaper, and an AM radio station. We had our share of professionals, including lawyers and doctors. Most folks were Baptist or Methodists, but the Catholics, Episcopalians and Presbyterians had beautiful churches and strong congregations. Our mayor, Harry Applebaum, was Jewish. The vast majority of the citizens were good, salt of the earth folks who worked hard for a meager living. The Jenkins, like many of the residents of Graball Hill, were not among Yazoo's aristocracy. We were striving to move up to lower class.

Spring and autumn are the best seasons. Summers are oppressively hot and humid, and winters can get very cold. Yazoo City gets at least one snowfall each year, sometimes a foot or more. Southerners have a fear of being snowed in by a blizzard, which must happen at least once every century. Actually, it snows two days each winter, ranging from a few giant snowflakes that melt the instant they hit the ground, to a respectable snowfall by standards for anyplace south of the Mason-Dixon Line. I don't know why it is so, but Southerners cannot drive in snow, and Californians cannot drive in rain. Having lived in both places, I can report that their lack of driving skills in inclement weather stop neither of them from trying. Once Woody Asaaf, the Jackson weatherman, said snow was on the way, everyone in Yazoo City headed for Fred's Dollar Store to stock up on…well, we were not sure what to stock up on for the coming blizzard. It was like church attendance: you were raised to show up at Fred's and stock up on...well, I can't remember what. No one wanted to look like the Yazoo Yokel by having to ask their neighbor for something they forgot to stock. That's when the pileups began (I mean the automobile kind, not the snow pileup).

Yazoo City is proud to have been home to some citizens who became successful and famous. They include: Jerry Clower, Country Music Hall of Fame comedian; Willie Morris, nationally recognized author who wrote about the town in many of his books, "My Dog Skip" became a popular movie; and Zig Zieglar, motivational speaker and writer. Haley Barbour was recently elected Governor, after having served as Chair of the Republican National Committee. Owen Cooper, industrialist and philanthropist, influenced many people's lives for the good, including the Jenkins. Mike Espy, Congressman and U.S. Secretary of Agriculture in the first Clinton administration, hails from Yazoo City.

Actress Stella Stevens was born there. Willie Brown, NFL Hall of Fame inductee, and Delta Blues legends Skip James and Tommy McClennan, called Yazoo City home. The list goes on. To have been a relatively small community, Yazoo City has the good fortune of having more than its share of noteworthy citizens.

CHAPTER 4

From Capitol Hill to Graball Hill

"He who knows how to be poor knows everything."
Jules Michelet

I grew up on a kudzu farm on Graball Hill near Yazoo City. Graball Hill overlooks the vast, flat, fertile Mississippi Delta. Small hills appear large next to the Delta flatlands, a rich and fertile region that runs from Memphis to Vicksburg. Daddy said you could push a marble at Memphis, and it would not stop rolling until it passed Vicksburg. That's how flat the Delta is. Traveling from the south or east through the Delta, Graball Hill looks like a mountain; but even anthills are given names in the Delta. Likewise, descending Broadway Hill into downtown Yazoo City after driving up from Jackson, you get the sensation of being dropped onto a vast tableau. Positioned at the line of demarcation between the hills and the Delta, Yazoo City became known as "The Gateway to the Delta". So, Yazooans can claim to be either "hillbillies" or "Delta rats."

Such designations were, and still are, important.

We didn't intend to be kudzu farmers. We wanted to grow corn, potatoes, tomatoes, okra, and such. But as every true Southerner knows, once kudzu takes hold, there's no escaping it. No matter what we planted, kudzu grew. So we reasoned, "If you can't beat it, join it." Becoming kudzu farmers assumed someone would find a useful purpose for the darn stuff. No one ever did. It is true that Otena Jones once started a business making baskets from dead kudzu vines, but her business, unlike the vine itself, never took off, mainly because dead kudzu vines were a lot harder to come by than live ones. Harvesting kudzu into bales, like hay, in the oppressive heat and humidity was backbreaking work. Once the kudzu harvest was completed, we stored it in the barn and hoped to sell it. That must be where my optimism came from, because only an optimist would hope to sell the dreaded green vine. Kudzu futures on the Chicago Board of Trade never got off zero, so we were poor—very poor.

So how did we get into this situation in the first place? I did a little investigation. Some folks call it genealogy, the science of collecting dead relatives. In the 1700s, my Jenkins ancestors settled in Virginia, in what is now the District of Columbia. They owned a plot of ground, called "Jenkins Hill". In 1790, the Jenkins sold the land to Pierre L'Enfant, who was charged with laying out the new nation's capital. L'Enfant said the parcel was a "pedestal waiting for a superstructure". The Federal Capitol Building was erected upon the crest of the hill, and the name quickly changed from Jenkins Hill to Capitol Hill. Thinking they had pulled one over on the Frenchman, the Jenkins took the money and headed to South Carolina, and then to Calhoun County, Mississippi, just in time for the Civil War.

The Civil War depleted whatever was left from the sale of Jenkins Hill. Decades of reconstruction and poverty, world wars, floods, and the depression were followed by more poverty. Then someone had an idea of planting kudzu to control soil erosion. The South would never be the same again.

My father was William Lester Jenkins. Mother's name is Martha Elizabeth Roberts Jenkins. Their parents called them Lester and Martha. We called them Pop and Mother. I am proud to have been named Junior after my father. Like almost all my ancestors for over 100 years, my parents were born in Calhoun County, in the north-central Mississippi hills, near Oxford. My parents left Calhoun County in their youth for the promise of a richer life and better soil in the northern Delta, near Clarksdale. What they found were swamps, floods, uncut forests, alligators, snakes, mosquitoes, oppressive heat, hard work, poverty, and the all too familiar kudzu. Pop's first wife, Fannie Mae, died young, leaving him the single parent of two daughters, Ellen and Linda. He ran a dry cleaning establishment with his brothers in Clarksdale. Mother was a farm girl in nearby Tunica County, just south of Memphis. Their paths crossed, and they married in 1939. They remained married until Pop died in 1989, just six weeks short of their Golden Anniversary.

After bouncing back and forth between Calhoun, Coahoma, and Quitman Counties, my parents arrived in Yazoo City in 1945 when Pop got a job driving a grader with the highway department. They rented a four-room shack with no indoor plumbing, plus an adjoining out house, barn and a few acres at the base of Graball Hill, located just outside the northern city limits of Yazoo City. I guess we qualified as tenant farmers. For sure, we qualified as poor. Our house sat almost at the foot of Graball Hill's western slope, but high enough to provide us with some spectacular sunsets. Yazoo City was and always will be home, no matter where I actually live.

Today, only the Yazoo old timers refer to this area as Graball Hill. From Graball's southern base, where Fifteenth

Street and Highway 49 intersect, to our home was a distance of a mile or more. In my childhood, I walked that mile a thousand times. In my boyhood days, it was nothing but fields, creeks, a pond, and farmland. Today, this area has been annexed into the city limits with scores of nice homes. Until a modern subdivision called Bella Vista began in 1958, our house, and one other shack, were the only residences on that side of Graball Hill. Several families lived over the crest of Graball Hill, and greatly influenced our lives growing up.

My parents soon found that, by moving to Yazoo City, they had neither outrun poverty nor the kudzu.

CHAPTER 5

Yazoo's Poorest "Million Dollar" Family

"I wasn't born in a log cabin, but my family moved into one as soon as they could afford it."
Melville D. Landon

We were poor. How poor were we? If another depression had struck in 1955, we would never have known it. There were nine of us: Pop, Mother, Ellen, Linda, Norman, Marietta, Tommy, me, and Louis, in that order. We lived in a four-room shack. That didn't count the extra room out back with the crescent moon on the door. I once asked Pop why he stayed in impoverished Mississippi. "I didn't know we were free to leave!" he replied. Our roots in Mississippi are as deep as the kudzu.

We may have been poor, but we were clean. I don't mean to brag, but we took a bath every Saturday, whether we needed it or not, in a round outdoor tub that we hung on the side of the house when we were finished with our weekly bathing ritual. In the winter, we didn't sweat as much, so we needed fewer baths. We heated up water on the wood-burning stove. I recall Mother stood next to the tub, giving each of us two minutes so the next in line would still have some warm water. Assembly line bathing, I guess you could call it. Being next to the youngest, I remember those winter baths were cold, short, and I was not sure if I was any cleaner coming out than going in. The Assured Brethren Church had a policy against "mixed bathing". Actually, I think it was a policy about boys and girls swimming together, but they called it mixed bathing. They were worried that if boys and girls frolicked in the water in little more than their skivvies, it might lead to dancing, and then you have real issues. I worried that we were in violation of church discipline on the mixed bathing ban.

The little red shack at the foot of Graball Hill was my first home, until we moved into town in 1959. Little red shack wasn't entirely accurate. The house carried only a hint of the red paint applied a decade before my parents arrived. They had neither the money nor the inclination to repaint it. I dreamed of the day I would live in a nice home, with bright white paint, like the mansions, or what I perceived to be mansions, I saw every day from the school bus along Grand Avenue or Broadway.

We had running water because I ran it back and forth from the cistern to the house. The bucket seemed as tall as me, and when filled with water, it was quite a burden for a seven year old. The cistern was located about a hundred feet from the house, just behind the chinaberry tree. Night treks to the cistern were often illuminated by the moonlight. Then we got a flashlight, which worked some of the time. A trough ran from the tin roof of the house down to the cistern to catch fresh rainwater. In the summertime, we would lower a ladder into the cistern and clean it. Lizards, snakes, sometimes frogs, would greet us as we scraped algae and slime off the brick walls of the cistern. We drank that water for years, and it never seemed to affect us…affect us…affect us. The pump needed priming before water would come up. Priming the pump creates a suction that forces the water up the pump shaft into the bucket. We all drank from the same dipper, a metal object with a cup on one end and a long handle, just like the Big Dipper constellation. It was a bad thing for anyone to drink the last water in the bucket, because about three or four dippers of water were needed to get the pump primed to draw up more water. But on a hot day, when we came in from the fields, we sometimes forgot, and drank the bucket dry. There would be no water from the cistern until a shower would bring us some new water designated for pump priming, or, we would walk a mile to Mrs. Crutcher's artesian well to get enough water to put us back into business.

It never failed that Mother or one of my sisters would dispatch me to go get another bucket of water after dark. Before the age of television, we would sit around the fireplace telling ghost stories, or listening to "The Shadow" on the radio. Just as the hair on my neck was standing at perfect attention, the order for a bucket of water would come. Then, for good measure, my oldest brother, Norman, would say, "Don't worry, Junior, (my childhood moniker), they don't think that escaped convict was heading in this direction." I would run to the well as fast as I could, pray that it would prime on the first try, and then race back to the house, absolutely sure I was just one step ahead of a vicious black panther who had not had a meal in three or four days. Inevitably, I would get back inside with only half a bucket full of water, although it was almost full when I left the cistern.

In the kitchen was a sink in which the dishes were cleaned, but when we released the water, it simply flowed out a pipe to the ground outside the house. Sometimes, we got water from the highway department shop, brought it home in a fifty-five-gallon barrel by a mule-drawn ground sled. Only half of the water made it to the house. Maybe the mule was afraid of panthers, too? When Pop got a tractor, he could pull the sled home. Tractors don't care about such things as escaped convicts and panthers, but some still spilled. That barrel of water was a blessing to us. Today, we may complain about the high cost of electricity and gasoline, but never the cost of having indoor plumbing, especially fresh cold water at the turn of a tap. It has always puzzled me that most Californians buy bottles of water when tap water is still a luxury to me.

Pop had a passion for politics. He campaigned for state and local candidates along his routes. Because he was respected, politicians liked Pop. He knew many people throughout the state. One day, at a political rally in Goose Egg Park, the governor came over to where we were standing. "Pop Jenkins, ol' buddy, how' you doing?' the governor said in a loud voice with a firm handshake. "Fine, Governor," Pop replied. "How's your ol' dad?" the governor asked. "He died," Pop said softly. "Oh, I'm sorry to hear that. He was a fine man." "Thank you," Pop said.

An hour or so later, the governor came back around, and apparently had shaken so many hands he forgot their earlier conversation. "Pop Jenkins, ol' buddy, how' you doing?" he asked again. "Fine, Governor," Pop replied again. "How's your ol' dad?" the governor asked.

Perplexed, Pop responded, "He's still dead."

Pop was a natural born salesman—he could sell a fly swatter to a mosquito. He sold automobiles at Valley Chevrolet in Yazoo City for decades. At my father's funeral, the minister contrasted Pop to Willie Lohman in the Broadway play, "Death of a Salesman". Pop and Willie were both natural salesmen. The difference was Willie was not a happy man. My Pop was happy, and content with his lot in life. Mostly, he seemed to be happy that he had a large family. "I may not have a dime," he often said, "but I have a 'million dollar' family." However, he was always quick to add, "I wouldn't give you a plug nickel for another one."

I was blessed to have an extended family in Yazoo City. My father was one of fifteen children, and eight of them lived long enough to play memorable roles in my early childhood. Pop's sister Minnie and her husband, Wilburn Cobb, lived in Yazoo City. I loved Aunt Minnie, because she had the best sense of humor, and could tell stories better than anyone I knew. Minnie weighed a good three hundred pounds. Wilburn, like my father, was 5'6" and weighed a bit over one hundred pounds, soaking wet. When Minnie and Wilburn stood side by side, I often wondered how they ever got together. I cannot remember Uncle Wilburn ever saying a word. After all, when you are married to Minnie Jenkins, there was no need to say anything. She said it all.

Mother's sister, Louise, also lived in Yazoo City for a while. She married Eddie Guice, and had four children. Mother's brother, Uncle Ed, visited us often as well. With a dozen aunts and uncles, we had cousins by the dozens who would stop by for visits.

As I said, we were poor. But when I stop to think about it, we were the richest family in Yazoo County. We were rich in the things money cannot buy: love, happiness, family, faith and health.

CHAPTER 6

I'm Telling Momma On You

"Happiness is having a large, loving, caring, close-knit family in another city."
George Burns (1896-1996)

Today, parents look upon childbirth as a liability; how much it will cost to care for and educate the little tyke. I heard one new father say, "Well, I'm now a half million dollars in debt, because that's what it will cost to rear and educate this baby." How sad! Many parents carefully plan when and where and how they will have their children. In the 1940s, parents saw babies as an asset; another strong back to help with the chores. Forget the cost of child rearing. Just pour some more water in the soup, and set another plate at the table. Just like a mother hog with a fine new litter at feeding time, each piglet has to learn to "root, hog, or die."

The King James Version of the Bible says, "*Lo, children are an heritage of the LORD: and the fruit of the womb is his reward.*" (Psalm 127:3). My parents were greatly rewarded.

Being part of a large, loving family is about the best thing that ever happened to me. Oh, sure, we had our differences growing up. We fought and we forgave. We were at the same time kind and hurtful. That was part of the journey. Such experiences prepare a child for the real world outside home. But no matter what we said or did, we knew that every one of our brothers and sisters were there for us in a time of need. We may have fought among ourselves, as siblings do, but if anyone from outside fought one of us, they had to fight all of us. It was the Code of Graball Hill.

We learned early the power of the phrase, "I'm telling Momma on you!" I was convinced Mother had eyes in the back of her head, although I never saw them. Mother, with all her chores and responsibilities, could not see and hear everything. After all, there were seven of us, and only one of her. Rarely, one of us would do something that would escape Mother's radar, such as when Tommy and I found a pack of cigarettes and smoked the whole pack behind the barn. My older sister Marietta had that same uncanny ability to know when we were up to no good. Maybe it's a female thing passed from mother to daughter. Anyway, Marietta tracked us down and caught us red handed, just as we were turning green from inhaling too much. I didn't know you were supposed to exhale. "I'm telling Momma on you!" she exclaimed. In a way, I was glad she caught us, because smoking was not all it was puffed up to be.

Once we got "told on" by one of our siblings, two things followed. One was a lesson in horticulture, although we didn't appreciate it as such at the time. Mother would instruct us to go get a switch from the peach tree. All the whippings Norman received alone should have killed the peach tree. But therein lies the lesson. It was called pruning. The more limbs we tore off the peach tree, the healthier it became. The second phase of our sentencing was the whipping itself. I know many people adhere to the philosophy that spanking children is child abuse. Having been the object of such discipline, I believe it made me a better person. I never felt abused, but always felt I was loved. Pop would sometimes say, "This whipping is going to hurt me more than you." I would respond, "Yeah, but not in the same place."

Ellen and Linda's mother died young. I guess that makes us half brothers and sisters, but there was never anything half way about our love for each other. Both Ellen and Linda learned early the reality of deprivation and hard work. In addition to chopping wood, carrying water, feeding the stock, working in the fields, and helping Mother with cooking, Ellen and Linda had the special privilege of changing dirty diapers and rocking crying babies who increased in number each year.

Ellen was the oldest. She was an angel. Her life was filled with adversity, but she never complained. Ellen knew that Mother needed help. There was a tenant family who lived about a quarter mile from our house. Linda was always a friendly, outgoing person, and loved to play with the little girl, Shirley, who lived there. They took turns being Roy Rogers and Dale Evans as they played their version of cowboys and cowgirls. But Linda had a bad habit of staying at the neighbor's house until after dark. This exhausted Mother's patience, so she developed a plan to get Linda home before dark, once and for all. Mother helped Ellen dress up like a ghost, and wait on a low limb of a chinaberry tree along the path between the two houses. Realizing she had played past dark again, Linda told Shirley, "I better get home." There were no streetlights, so Linda relied on her memory of the path, and ran as fast as she could toward the lights of our house. Just as Linda passed underneath the chinaberry tree, Ellen jumped down and roared like a monster. Linda was already a fast runner, but that night, the sky lit up like a lightning storm when Linda set a new world's record for the remaining 100-yard dash to our front door. I remember seeing Linda's blurred image rocketing through the house. The problem was Linda didn't have good brakes. She knocked Norman flat on his back, tore the screen off the kitchen door, and didn't stop until she hit the wire pigpen fence in the back yard. Wire fences make a funny noise when they get stretched. Linda didn't think it was as funny as I did, but she never played past dark, either.

The statute of limitations has long since expired, so the truth can now be told. Linda is an arsonist. Yes, my dear, saintly sister is responsible for the great fire of 1955 that burned the northern ridge of Graball Hill. It was an accident, but the result was frightening. In the days before waste management, we threw our rubbish into a garbage pile near the house. When the pile got big, we burned it. I am not sure if that was environmentally correct, but we were not members of the Green Party. One day, Linda decided it was time to burn the garbage pile. Once a year or so, we would scrape up the ashes and haul them away, and start a new pile. This was a necessary ritual that kept the garbage pile from becoming too large. On this particular day, Linda started a fire that spilled over into the dry weeds nearby. Before we knew it, the whole side of Graball Hill was ablaze. We grabbed shovels and sheets off the clothesline in a desperate attempt to control the blaze. All our swatting and pounding was not able to contain the blaze.

As I sat there, watching the blaze grow larger, climbing our side of Graball Hill faster than I remember ever running up it, several thoughts came to mind. I wondered what the Calhouns were doing that morning. Boy, were they going to be surprised when they looked out their windows and saw the fire topping the hill. I'll bet they weren't going to be too happy with Linda as they watched their homes, livestock, and family treasures going up in smoke. It's funny what you think about at a time like that.

That's when I learned a new lesson about kudzu. At the

top of the hill, there was a healthy line of new kudzu growth. It had covered the trees and set up a perimeter in its latest assault on Graball Hill. The fire burned right up to the kudzu, realized the futility of taking on the voracious vine, and burned itself out, as though it was tired from racing up Graball Hill. We have long since forgiven Linda of this misdemeanor, for those of us who are not without sin cannot cast stones.

There are people in Yazoo City who think my sister Linda cannot drive. Actually, Linda is an excellent driver. I saw her do one of the finest jobs of driving ever recorded in the days before NASCAR. Norman got a new bicycle for Christmas. By summer, the bike was well broken in. Norman and Tommy liked to do dare devil stunts by riding the bike down Graball Hill, and hitting the brakes just in time to avoid running across Highway 49. Linda said, "Let me try, let me try." Norman finally relented, and said, "If you hurt yourself, don't blame me." With the waiver of liability in hand, Norman held the bike as Linda got on, and started down the steep slope. Just as Linda was nearing the base of the hill, Norman yelled, "Now hit the brakes!" She did, but Linda's chain broke. If that had happened to Norman, he would have ditched the bike in the mud at the bottom of the hill, taking the scrapes and bruises like a man. Not so with Linda. She squealed with excitement as the wind blew in her face. She astutely steered the bike between two eighteen wheelers as she crossed Highway 49, and ducked her head to pick up steam as she flew across Mr. Grizzard's cornfield. She soon tired of the excitement, and wanted to stop, but she could not. Somewhere near Wolf Lake, Rev. Goodbody was performing an outdoor wedding for Ovenia Spinster and Bubba Jones, IV. Ovenia was an "unclaimed blessing," a Southern phrase for a less than beautiful unmarried woman. We were all surprised and pleased she had finally caught herself a man. Just as the preacher came to the phrase, "If anyone knows any reason why this man and this woman should not be united in holy matrimony," my sister Linda flew between the preacher and the couple. "Stop this thing, in the name of Heaven, stop this thing right now!" Linda screamed at the top of her lungs. Rev. Goodbody had not learned in seminary what to do if anyone ever objected. We received a phone call about an hour later from the Rolling Fork police that we could come pick up our sister and what was left of the bicycle. So driving was not a problem for Linda; brakes were a problem for Linda. In the interest of public safety, Linda chose to end her driving career that day in Rolling Fork. They named a street Bicycle Lane on Graball Hill in honor of my sister's famous adventure. Lance Armstrong would have been proud.

Norman was the first child born to my mother and father. Being the oldest carries with it joys and trials. I think Norman got more than his share of whippings. The rest of us said Norman wore Pop and Mother down for us. Such is the lot of an oldest child. There was the time Norman was sent to get some hams out of the corncrib, a place we stored salt cured meat along with dried corn for the hogs and cows. Snakes found the crib a particularly good place to escape the Mississippi sun. Norman didn't like going to the crib in the first place, but when Dominic, the Rhode Island red rooster saw him coming, Norman knew he was in for a challenge. Roosters can be very territorial, and no matter what Norman did, the rooster would not let Norman pass by to the crib. We used to play "Red Rover, Red Rover, Send Norman Right Over" and Norman had some good moves, but Dominic had seen them all. Dominic had a few good moves of his own. Norman came back to the house without a ham. This was whipping number 147.

We had a mule named Jake. Like most mules, Jake was stubborn. Pop tried to teach Jake to "gee" and "haw" but like Dominic the rooster, he had a mind and will all his own.

The angriest I ever saw my father was when Jake refused to "gee" while pulling the plow. Pop had enough, and slugged Jake just like that guy in "Blazing Saddles". I mean Pop gave Jake a left hook that stunned the mule temporarily, but did nothing to improve either Pop or Jake's disposition. Norman said, "Why don't you get a tractor?" The next day, Pop came driving up the road on a very old tractor he bought for ten dollars. Norman was thrilled, and learned to drive the tractor. The only problem was that the tractor had to cross a ditch to get into the field. Norman came up with a plan to jump the ditch. He drove the tractor right up to the edge of the ditch, revved up the engine, and popped the clutch. The tractor jumped like a bullfrog, and almost made it across the ditch. Almost! That was whipping number 273.

My father owned the Snow White Cleaners in Yazoo City. It was a family business where we worked after school and Saturdays until Pop sold the business when I was very young. Norman stole a pack of Camel cigarettes from the lady who ran the steam press. Norman's first experiment with smoking resulted in the press padding catching on fire. That was whipping number 298; the one Norman still refers to as his worst whipping ever.

But Norman is a great older brother. Unfortunately for him, we look almost like twins. It worked to my advantage when Norman went off to Mississippi State. Norman and two friends, Wiley Barbour and Shad Arnold, were coming through Yazoo City on their way to the Mississippi State - Florida football game at Memorial Stadium. They asked if I wanted to go. No hesitation there. On the way to Jackson, I asked where my ticket was. Norman said not to worry; he had a plan. Students got in free with their photo ID. Norman told me to stand near the fence, while he, Shad, and Wiley went through the gate. Norman circled around, came back to the fence and passed his ID through to me. I got to sit in the MSU student section and watch my first college football game. The maroon jerseys looked amazing against the greenest grass I had ever seen, and there was no kudzu. Florida had a new quarterback named Steve Spurrier. The students chanted, "Go to heck Ole Miss, go to heck." I asked Norman why the students were chanting against Ole Miss when we were playing Florida. He said, "You will learn." And so I did. Sometimes my conscience bothers me about sneaking into that game. But the memories are wonderful, and I wouldn't have missed it for anything. And beside, I can rationalize that MSU got a lifelong fan out of the deal.

Half way between our house and Fifteenth Street was a railroad bridge, or trestle. Our parents warned us never to walk across the trestle. If a train suddenly appeared, there would be no time to race across. We would either have to jump into the creek below, or get run over by the locomotive. However, the railroad route was shorter than following the highway, so Norman taught us how to tempt fate on the railroad bridge. I often imagined, while walking quickly across the railroad trestle, what would happen if I got my shoe caught between the rails? Would the locomotive be able to stop in time? That's why Mother said, "Do not get on the trestle". And that's why we found it such an exciting adventure. Walking across the trestle accounted for whippings 130, 187, 204, and 228.

By the time Marietta came along, Ellen and Linda were getting on with their lives, so Marietta inherited the least coveted job of helping raise four less than perfect brothers. I have to give her credit; she did a pretty good job. I would never have admitted it, because most of the time I was reminding her that she was not my mother, and therefore challenging her authority to assign me chores. At least I tried. Marietta was an expert on using the "I'm going to tell Momma on you" line...and the peach tree grew stronger.

Tommy was just a year older than me. He invented a mnemonic way to write his name. "Down, cross (T), little round ball (O), up down, up down (M), up down, up down (M), down, up, down (Y)," Tommy would chant as he spelled out his name mnemonically. Years later I heard someone singing a song in which they spelled, M-I-crooked letter, crooked letter-I-crooked letter, crooked letter-I-hump back, hump back-I. (MISSISSIPPI)." I felt like they should have given Tommy a royalty for using his mnemonic method of spelling.

Tommy liked firecrackers, even though they were forbidden without appropriate adult supervision. One day, Tommy brought a package of cherry bombs home. "Want to go with me to shoot off these firecrackers?" he asked me. "Sure, but won't we get into trouble?" I asked. "You sissy," he said. That always worked so I went with him down to the pecan trees where he would light one, hold it as long as he could, and then throw it in the air. The cherry bomb would explode in mid air, just above our heads. "You better not hold on too long or it will explode in your hand," I said. After all, what are little brothers good for if not offering advice? "You sissy," he said again. Then he lit another one, but the fuse wasn't just right. It let off a hissing sound, and Tommy immediately threw it straight up in the air. We watched it hiss as it went up in the air and as it fell...right into Tommy's shoe. The cherry bomb lodged next to his ankle between his foot and the shoe. At first, he started to pull it out, but he was afraid it would explode in his hand. So Tommy began stomping his foot in hopes of shaking the cherry bomb out of his shoe. I never saw anyone stomp as hard and as fast as Tommy did. He stomped down a perfect circle in the garden before the cherry bomb finally exploded. Luckily, the bomb, like the fuse, was a dud. It scared him more than it hurt him. That is the story of Yazoo City's first crop circle. We told our parents and friends the crop circle was probably formed by an alien space ship. There must be a lot of kids playing with fireworks, because years later, crop circles appeared all over the world. Tommy and I knew how they got there.

Louis was the youngest, and the only family member younger than me. Louis was an industrious person, even when he was young. I remember the Friday night we went to "Klondike" at the Yazoo Theater. Klondike was a marketing strategy to get people to attend the movies. Klondike was usually a double feature movie and during the intermission, there was a drawing for a jackpot. If the person was present, he or she won the jackpot. That particular night, Louis and I were playing Siskel and Ebert, critiquing the first movie, "Bye, Bye Birdie". Over Louis' commentary about Ann Margret's performance, I heard the usher say, "And our Klondike winner is…Louis Jenkins." "Louis, Louis! You won." I said. "Oh sure," he replied, and continued his train of thought about how Ann was too good for the role. "Is Louis Jenkins here?" the usher asked in a noticeably louder voice. I stood up and said, "I am not Louis, but he is right here." Louis finally stood up and received the applause of everyone in attendance. He won $1300, not bad for showing up at a movie! I think Louis may still have that $1300. I think he asked for the Ann Margret poster, too. Actually, he probably invested the jackpot in the stock market and, just like kudzu, watched it grow. Louis lives by the motto, "The harder I work, the luckier I get."

CHAPTER 7

T-Baby, Shinky, Beakie, and Snake

"Nicknames stick to people, and the most ridiculous are the most adhesive."
Thomas Chandler Haliburton

What ever happened to the great old country names? Southern names have a unique charm. I am not talking about the elegant, genteel Southern names on an Atlanta plantation, like Aloysius Barksdale Beauregard, or Jackson Clayton Lauderdale. I am talking about good old homemade country Southern names. Billy Bob and Mary Lou are mere stereotypes. Let me tell you about some classic names of the citizens on Graball Hill. Some of the names were nicknames, but others were real. Even the nicknames became so established that if you mailed a letter with the person's legal name on it, the letter would be returned annotated "addressee unknown". Our Southern names reflect our history and culture.

Beakie Buzzard

Now, that's a great Southern name. There actually was a fellow on Graball Hill named Beakie Buzzard. I think his real name was Trey Hawke. His friends nicknamed him, to enhance his image. With friends like that, who needs enemies? Beakie could spit chewin' tobacco without opening his mouth. The legends about Beakie are many. One day Beakie's friends were in a rather playful mood. They decided to play like Beakie was their horse. So when they stopped at a store on Graball Hill to get a few beers, they tied a rope around Beakie's neck. They tied the other end to the rear bumper of their pickup truck. "Now Trigger," they said to Beakie, "you stay right here until we get back." The guys went into the store and had a bit more than a few beers. Trigger, I mean Beakie, got tired and hot, so he sat down beside the truck, waiting for his friends to return. When they came out, I don't know if it was because of their inebriation or that they forgot they tied Beakie to the bumper. They jumped into the pickup and sped off down the steep dusty road. One thing is certain; Beakie was a fast thinker, and an even a faster runner. Before the slack in the rope was gone, Beakie fell in behind the pickup and started running as fast as he could. The fellows in the truck turned the radio up as loud as it would go, and never heard Beakie yelling for help. Passersby report that Beakie never lost the slack in the rope. If it were not for the stop sign at the foot of Graball Hill, Beakie might still be chasing that pickup.

Shinky Newberry

Or was it Nuberry? Rarely did anyone take off points for misspelling on Graball Hill. Anyway, this was another of the great old Southern names. Whether this was a real name, or another one of those favors the guys' friends do for him, I do not know. I suspect that Shinky got his mail addressed to Shinky Newberry, because with a nickname like that, who would ever remember his real name? On the fourth Saturday afternoon of each month, we held pig races on Graball Hill. Folks came from places like Rolling Fork, Holly Bluff, Silver City and Satartia, to enter their best boars and sows in the races. Shinky had a prize hog named Jubal, who wore the champion's belt for as long as I can remember. Shinky was proud of that hog, and agreed with what Winston Churchill once said, ""I like pigs. Dogs look up to us. Cats look down on us. Pigs treat us like equals." I can testify that Jubal had no equal. Our prize hog Shadrack once came in second, but never beat Jubal Newberry.

Turkey and Snake Hawkins

Now we enter the realm of the more practical names. The Hawkins were one of the more prominent families on Graball Hill. These, I can say with some degree of certainty, were nicknames. How would anyone get a name like Turkey or Snake? Those of us who possess Southern culture know how these things happen. Probably Turkey had some unfortunate experience with a turkey, and the way his friends reminded him of this was by naming him Turkey. This served a dual purpose. Not only did it give Turkey a nickname, it reminded his friends of that unfortunate event, probably something very embarrassing, every time they called his name. The first hundred or so times his friends called him Turkey, his face got real red, and he would get angry. But after a while, he started getting used to it, and even liked it, and the rest, as they say, is history. You know that a nickname is established when your mother uses it. "Where is Leonard?" "Who? Oh, you mean MudCat. He's down at the pond, fishing." The folks up on Graball Hill had a real liking for bird names, like Beakie Buzzard and Turkey. Since I have a natural aversion to snakes, I don't even want to speculate how Snake got his name.

T-Baby Calhoun

My favorite family on Graball Hill was the Calhoun family. And they had some of the best names, real or nick! The most vivid of these was T-Baby Calhoun. Maybe it was spelled Tee-Baby, but the correct pronunciation was to emphasize the Tee. T-Baby was a fighter. The Calhouns were, as we say in the South, "bad news". T-Baby was proud when folks called him a "hood," because he thought that meant he was like James Dean in "Rebel Without a Cause". He slicked his hair back like Elvis, and rolled a pack of cigarettes up in his tee shirt sleeve. No one on Graball Hill messed with T-Baby. But when some poor unfortunate soul ventured up Graball Hill, and after a few beers decided to fight, it had better not be with T-Baby Calhoun. Give T-Baby credit, though. He always warned his opponents, "Don't mess with me, I'm T-Baby Calhoun." If the unsuspecting intruder on Graball Hill came from anywhere in Yazoo County, he surely would have heard of T-Baby. He would know that discretion is the better part of valor, and a prompt exit off Graball Hill would be in order. I even used it to get out of a couple tight spots, "Hey, don't mess with me. I'm T-Baby Calhoun." No one ever wanted to fight with me after I said that. Then one day I saw this particularly fearsome looking dude. "Hey, don't mess with me. I'm T-Baby Calhoun," I said. The real T-Baby whipped my tail right then and there for using his name and famous line. Over time, T-Baby and I developed a strange and wonderful relationship. Of course, I was wonderful, and he was strange. But T-Baby and I shared many adventures, some of which I am going to take to my grave. I keep thinking one day I'll run into him again, and I'm so old now, I don't think I can take another tail whipping.

Booger and Booger Dee

Then there was Booger Calhoun and his son, Booger Dee.

This is another way Southerners get some of the great names. When you finally get a really great name, like Booger, you don't want it to die out in just one generation. So you just pass it along to your offspring, with the appropriate appendage. The Calhouns were good at this. Booger Dee works. But something like Booger Lee, or Booger Joe would never work. This is another way of knowing who has class. Some say Booger Dee was the Mayor of Graball Hill. Since Graball Hill is unincorporated, I doubt it. But because Booger Dee and T-Baby were related, I also never challenged it.

There were other great names around Graball Hill and Yazoo County. One fellow was named Bird Legs. We even had a mayor of Yazoo City named Harry Applebaum. But I was fifteen years old before I found out his name was not Apple Bomb. My high school principal was a good man, known as "Hard Rock" Kelly. I don't think the Rock had anything to do with rock and roll, which was becoming popular among Yazoo City's youth about that time.

Even my own family was not immune to nicknames. Norman was called "Big 'Un" because he was six foot five by the time he was fourteen; Tommy was aptly named "Hot Rod" because he loved drag racing in his Corvette; I was known as "Junior", which was fine with me because the alternative was my Daddy's middle name, Lester; and Louis was labeled "Lewis", but no one ever figured that one out.

I acquired another nickname from my friends in high school, "Bean Pole", because I was tall and skinny. How skinny was I? I was so skinny I could turn sideways and the teacher would mark me absent. I was so skinny I had to jump around in the shower to get wet. I was so skinny that I could stand under a clothesline in a thunderstorm and stay dry. Life plays a trick on men when they get to a certain age. No one has called me Bean Pole in a long, long, long time.

I hope Yazoo City is still coming up with great old Southern nicknames.

CHAPTER 8

Topey, the Righteous Wonder Dog

"It's not the size of the dog in the fight;
it's the size of the fight in the dog."
Mark Twain (1835-1910)

Topey (pronounced TOE-pee), became part of my family before I did. Like most dogs around Graball Hill, he had mixed ancestry. Canine genealogy wasn't a big deal in Yazoo City in the 1950s. Topey was mostly Mississippi bulldog, with a little German shepherd and a pinch of pit bull thrown in for good measure. Topey considered himself not a pet, but a family member, as indeed he was. I cannot remember a scene from my early childhood when Topey was not present.

Topey was a great outfielder. I pitched, Louis was the catcher, Tommy batted, and Norman was the infielder. Without Topey in the outfield, our kudzu league baseball games would have been very short in the hot Delta sun. Topey could chase down a line drive, leap, and catch the ball with his mouth. He rarely muffed a grounder, and could tag Tommy out unassisted before he reached third base. His batting average was lousy, but with an outfielder like Topey, who cared? When the Calhouns came over the hill, and we had enough players to chose sides, Topey was always the first selected. The Calhoun's mutt, Poochie, was dumb as a stick, and never understood the finer points of the game, such as the infield fly rule.

Even as a young boy, I wanted to be a minister and I knew Topey was a righteous dog, because I practiced my first baptism ceremonies on him. He loved being in the water as much as pigs love mud. We had a wayward cat called "Shugga". I think her name may have been "Sugar" but we never saw the name in writing, only heard it from our folks, and so we always called her Shugga. She and her kittens would not allow me to baptize them. Topey and I suspected they had Presbyterian leanings. Topey loved attending church with us. He knew Sundays were different from other days. The first clue: Pop didn't go to work. My sisters wore their Sunday dresses, while Tommy, Louis, and I took turns wearing out Mother's patience. Topey would jump through the open car window and honk the horn until we ceased our foolishness. The whole family crammed into the car. How did we get nine people in one car? Not easily—four in the front, and five in the back, with the little ones sitting on the laps of the "big 'uns".

Topey attended Sunday school with us at the Assured Brethren Church. His favorite Sunday School activity was crafts, when we got on the floor to color and paste Bible pictures. When worship time followed, Topey took his usual seat, or should I say floor, in the church foyer. Topey joined in when we sang. He was somewhere between a baritone and a tenor. When Rev. Goodbody got fired up in his sermon, and the deacons began with their "Amens", Topey barked his approval. We knew Rev. Goodbody was having a bad day if Topey was completely silent.

On one particularly hot Sunday, Rev. Goodbody was doing an unusually good job preaching about demons. Shugga, our wayward cat, just happened to be in the neighborhood and decided to walk into church to see what was going on. Shugga was a roamer. She would disappear for weeks at a time and we didn't know where she went, but wherever it was, she always brought back lots of kittens. As Ernest Hemingway said, "One cat just leads to another." We didn't mind, because the more cats we had (baptized or not), the fewer mice we had in the woodpile. At first, Shugga and Topey did not see each other. Then there was an awkward moment when their eyes locked. Dogs believe they are human. Cats believe they are God. Topey was convinced Shugga was a Presbyterian, and had only shown up to cause trouble. I don't know what came over me, but I leaned down toward Topey, and in a quiet voice said, "Sic 'em." You don't say "Sic 'em" to a Mississippi bulldog unless you are prepared for action.

Shugga took off running underneath the pews down the left side of the church. She was making an awful sound, wailing like a banshee. Topey was close behind, growling like a demon, which fit beautifully with Rev. Goodbody's sermon. Imagine sitting in church, minding your own business, and two furry demons run between your legs. Those of us sitting on the right side of the church could see the commotion as the ripple worked its way toward the front of the church, with startled people jumping slightly up off their pews. We thought they were getting religion, and for some of them, it was about time.

Aunt Minnie, my dad's sister, and Uncle Wilburn watched the spectacle from the right side of the church. Aunt Minnie had her funeral home fan, made out of a piece of cardboard with the local funeral home advertisement on it, connected to a giant popsicle stick. As the demons got closer to the front of the church, Shugga made a strategic decision to take a sharp right and run back toward the foyer, this time down the right side of the church. Aunt Minnie watched the commotion coming toward her, and started fanning herself faster, saying, "Wilburn! Wilburn! Do something, Wilburn!"

What happened next is a bit of a blur. As best I recall, Shugga decided to run up the inside of Aunt Minnie's two-dollar, black and white polka-dot dress, followed closely by Topey. Minnie squalled; "Help me, help me, Jesus!" convinced a demon had attacked her. As Topey and Shugga continued their chase, running around between Aunt Minnie's knees, Uncle Wilburn allowed himself a chuckle—he had never seen Minnie move like that before! In a desperate attempt to be rid of the curse, Minnie began confessing her sins aloud, punctuated with cries of "Forgive me, Jesus!" As a seven year old boy, I didn't understand everything she said, but was impressed Aunt Minnie was capable of some of those sins she confessed. However, when she ran out of her sins, she started confessing Uncle Wilburn's sins, and that's when Rev. Goodbody prayed a quick but fervent prayer to close the service. Less than half the original congregation was left inside the church anyhow. Some, fearing demon attacks of their own, jumped out the open windows. Others, fearing Aunt Minnie would begin confessing their sins, bolted out the front door. When the congregation returned for evening services, the choir director was found still hiding in the baptistery.

Topey took his protector role very seriously. He saved every one of our lives at one time or another. My turn came one day when Topey and I went to the Old North Pond. This was the same pond I used for my practice baptizing. It was a usual hot Mississippi summer day, so I moved around the pond's edge to find shade under the old Bo-dock tree. Suddenly, something flew past my head, and I heard a splash at the pond's edge near my feet. Then I heard another splash as Topey dived on top of the largest Cottonmouth moccasin I have ever seen. Apparently, the snake, taking a siesta on a low hanging limb, decided I made a likely target, and took a leap at me. The snake bit Topey on the neck, but despite the injury, Topey killed him. Topey ran home, ignoring my calls, crawled under the house, and stayed there for several days without food or water. Pop crawled up under the house as far as he could, and reported Topey's neck was twice its normal size. We feared he would die. Perhaps because snakes before had bitten him, Topey's immunity saved him. Or maybe the Lord smiled on the often-baptized Topey. But he finally emerged from underneath the house, and I gave Topey, the righteous wonder dog, a hug and kiss for saving my life. Topey laughed by wagging his tail. He must have been a happy dog, and he certainly made our lives happier.

Dogs live too fast and die too soon. The Bible says heaven is a place where the lion lays down next to the lamb. That must mean Topey is up there, still chasing butterflies and taking a swim in the river. Wait by the pond, old boy; we'll catch up with you soon.

CHAPTER 9

The First Day At School

"Going to call him 'William'? What kind of a name is that? Every Tom, Dick, and Harry is called William. Why not call him Bill?"
Samuel Goldwyn

My parents moved to Yazoo City in 1945 because they wanted to give their children the best educational opportunities possible. When we went through the Yazoo City public school system, it was indeed among the finest in the state, if not the nation. Whether we liked it or not, we were going to be the first on our side of the family tree to go to college.

Pop went through the eighth grade in the Scoona one-room schoolhouse in Calhoun County, with many of his brothers and sisters. All students were required to recite a verse each Friday. The verse could come from Shakespeare, literature, the Bible, or it could be an original composition. "Lester," Aunt Minnie asked my dad one Friday, "do you have your verse memorized for today?" Pop, who was known for his procrastination, replied "Don't worry. I have composed an original poem." "You better not be joking," Aunt Minnie said, "or you will get a whippin' when you get home". When time came for the students to recite their verses, Pop waited to be the very last speaker. Even as a boy, Pop was comfortable in front of a crowd. Because of his short stature, he stood on a table top in front of all eight grades, including his brothers and sisters.

"An original poem by Lester Jenkins entitled 'The Woodpecker'," Pop began with a mischievous grin.

> "*Woodpecker, woodpecker,*
> *Pecking on the door.*
> *Pecked so hard that*
> *His pecker got sore.*"

Pop jumped down off the table, and ran out the door as though his tail was on fire, (which it was, as soon as Aunt Minnie reported his antics to Grandma Jenkins). His career as a poet came to an end that day.

Mother went through the tenth or eleventh grade in Tunica County, where her parents moved after they left Calhoun County. She met my father and got married. Mother later received her GED and was a teaching assistant at Yazoo City for many years, a job she dearly loved.

Being next to the youngest, my first day at Annie Ellis Elementary School on Grand Avenue was an adventure and a life changing experience. I literally came home a different person after just one day. Since my brother Tommy was in the second grade, and sister Marietta was in the fourth grade, Mother felt there was no need to accompany me that first day. Norman was starting Junior High, and Linda was in High School. Ellen had already graduated, and was off at nurse's school. Mother gave me a bit of information before we met the school bus that notable day. She informed me that my name was not exactly 'Junior Jenkins'. I should respond if the teacher called out 'William Jenkins', because that was my real name. This was news to me! For six years, I had been comfortable with the identity of Junior Jenkins, and now, I experienced my first identity crisis, just as I was walking out the door for my first day of class! William Lester Jenkins, Junior. That was, and still is, my real name. I could see from the beginning that education was going to change many of my conceptions, but I was more deeply concerned about what else my mother had never told me. Was I adopted? Was there really a Santa Claus? What other earth shaking truths were floating around out there?

We Jenkins kids caught the school bus on Highway 49 at the end of the long, muddy road that served as our driveway. Today, that driveway is Twentieth Street. Our house sat near what is today the corner of Twentieth and Woodlawn Avenue, facing Highway 49. The bus was appropriately named and marked the "Minnie Mouse." This, I found out later, was to keep unsophisticated children like me from getting on the wrong bus and winding up at the wrong house. I often wondered what it would be like to accidentally go home with the Graebers, or the Coopers. Would they notice that I wasn't one of them? Would I get a nice room of my own? Maybe I *was* adopted (the security of a six year old is very fragile). But I digress. The other busses were named Mickey, Goofy (a rather unfortunate name for children seeking an education), Donald, and then they started with the seven dwarfs. At least my bus was not named Dopey. But all I had to remember was my bus was named Minnie, like my aunt, and if I got on it after the last bell rang, I would find my way back to Graball Hill, and Mother's fried chicken supper.

I followed Tommy and Marietta into the Annie Ellis school auditorium. It was the biggest room I had ever seen, even bigger than the sanctuary at the Assured Brethren Church. Then, there were classrooms, each larger than our entire house, and winding hallways that reminded me of Collins Cave on the backside of Graball Hill. I wondered how many children walked through those doors, got lost, and were never heard from again? I sat near the back of the auditorium in apprehension and wonder at my new surroundings.

Miss Harris was the principal at Annie Ellis. She explained that she was going to ask each teacher, one at a time, to stand near the front of the auditorium. Miss Harris would then call the names of students who would walk forward and stand next to their new surrogate mother. When the class roster was complete, that teacher would walk her students to their classroom, which looked like a mother duck followed by two dozen ducklings, and their education would begin. I sat forward in my seat, waiting to hear either Junior Jenkins or William Jenkins. Actually, I was kind of proud of having two names—Junior and William. It sort of made me feel like Superman with an alter-ego of Clark Kent. Miss Harris started with the first grade, which had three classes. The first teacher, Miss Johnson, stood near the front. I waited impatiently, hoping my name was on her list, because she was very pretty. I discovered that day I was not good at luck. The next teacher, Miss Cunningham, gathered her brood of students, and disappeared with them down the long hallway. Now, I was getting nervous, because I had only one more chance left to get an education. Incredibly, my name wasn't called for Miss Raynor's class, either. I thought to myself, "Don't panic. Maybe I haven't been forgotten. Maybe they are going to let me skip first grade, and start in the second grade." That would have made my brother, Tommy, upset after all the work he had to do to get promoted to second grade. The theory of advanced placement was plausible, but came crashing down as all three second-grade classes exited the auditorium, without William or Junior Jenkins. I had no choice but to sit there, and held up pretty well until my sister Marietta left with the fourth graders. Even T-Baby Calhoun, who had taken the second grade three times, was promoted to third grade. When Miss Harris called the last name for the last sixth grade class, I sat alone in the auditorium, no longer able to hold back my tears. I knew my parents wanted me to get an education, but it looked like from day one I was not going to make the grade, so to speak. Miss Harris came over to where I was sitting and said, "Little boy, what is your name?" "Junior Jenkins", I blurted out between sobs. "Mother told me to answer to William Jenkins, but you didn't call William or Junior." She scanned her roster, and said; "I think I have a class for you, Bill". That's right, she had called my name, but no one told me 'Bill' was a nickname for William. I was so confused—three names? But also relieved. She put her arm around me, and walked me down to Miss Cunningham's room, where I received a formal introduction to my new teacher and classmates, and began my educational odyssey.

I was relieved to see that Bobby David Roberts was in my class. Bobby David and I went to the Assured Brethren Church, and our families were good friends. The Roberts family was almost a carbon copy of the Jenkins, with a corresponding child of the same age and gender for each of us. Jackie, the oldest Roberts girl, was a good match for Ellen, Linda and Marietta. They did girl stuff, that didn't interest me much at the time. Then, if my memory serves me correctly, Van Roberts and Norman were about the same age, followed by Carl and Donald Roberts who were about Tommy's age, Bobby David was my best buddy, and Charles Roberts was Louis' age. The Roberts lived on Seventh Street, about two miles from our house on Graball Hill. We loved it when all the Roberts boys came over to our house, because we had enough players to make up a decent game of baseball. Topey had that sixth sense, and would run get his baseball glove a half hour before the Roberts arrived.

Bobby David and I spent the night at each other's house frequently. We got along wonderfully, but would occasionally have little disagreements that would end up with Bobby David saying, "My dad can beat up your dad." I knew he was right, since Pop was only five feet, six inches tall, and weighed about 130 pounds soaking wet. Pop lost an eye in an accident when he was a child. My only comeback to Bobby David was, "Oh yeah, I'll bet your dad can't pop his eyeball out at night." That usually ended the argument. It was an amazing sight to watch my father take his glass eye out at night, placing it on the nightstand next to his bed. Bobby David loved to sleep over at my house just to watch Pop as he went through this nightly ritual with his glass eye.

Elementary school was where I established myself as Yazoo City's first fashion maven. Today's youth think they developed the "hip hop" style of loose baggy pants, hanging down to display their unmentionables. Heck, I was wearing that in the 1950s—it was called hand-me-downs. I wore Tommy's clothes, which of course had been handed down from Norman. Their outgrown pants were not particularly suited to my skinny, hipless frame, and so, to my embarrassment, my teachers and classmates were frequently treated to glimpses of my BVDs. I never dreamed it would take nearly fifty years for that style to catch on.

The height of my fashion awareness occurred in second grade as a result of my first exposure as a performer. All three of the second grade classes joined together to stage a production of "A Mid Summer Night's Dream." I was cast as one of six elves. The teacher sent a pattern for my costume home with me. Mother created my costume perfectly, which was not difficult for her because, like her mother, my Mother was an expert seamstress. The outfit was brown, had a jester's collar, and covered me from head to toe. The only part of my body you could see was my face through a hole in the headpiece. The sock-like foot coverings curled up past my toes, and had tiny bells at the tip. I jingled as I walked. It was magic, and I thought adorable; and sure beat the ill-fitting, hand-me-down clothes I regularly wore. I really never minded wearing the hand-me-downs from Tommy. But when Tommy suggested I wear Marietta's old dresses, I drew the line.

The play was a big hit. I wore my outfit home on the bus. Many of my classmates offered their compliments on my outfit, something they had never done before, and I enjoyed the attention. When I got home, I told Mother I wanted to wear my elf suit again. She laughed and said absolutely not. What a shame I thought, for all that effort just for one wearing. The next day, I rolled the outfit up in my book bag and took it with me to school. I changed into my elf costume as soon as I arrived. I can honestly say I was the only student at Annie Ellis Elementary that day in an elf outfit. Somehow, my classmates didn't appreciate the avant garde, androgynous statement my elf suit made, especially since there was no Shakespeare production that day. T-Baby stopped me in the hall, called me a sissy, and proceeded to give me one of his famous whippings. That ended my short-lived career as a fashion trendsetter, and I went back to the boys' room to change into my hand-me-down clothes, which I appreciated much more after that day.

Bobby David and I were in the same homeroom for the first four years at Annie Ellis. Then, in 1959, my family moved into a house on Williams Street at the north end of Canal. It had indoor plumbing, a gas stove, and a refrigerator. No more pumping water, chopping kindling wood, and cold outdoor baths. I still remember the first bath I took indoors. It was as though we had left one universe and entered another. I discovered that because of the move, I was being transferred to Main Street Elementary School, five blocks from my new home, for my fifth and sixth grades, leaving my life long friends behind. But there were new friends and adventures at Main Street. Bobby David and my friends from both Annie Ellis and Main Street were reunited at Yazoo City Junior High, a few blocks west of my new home, when we began our seventh grade school year. The high school was only two blocks away, so from grade five to graduation, I walked to school. I made many friends in the Yazoo City schools, some of whom I still run into when I travel back to Old Yazoo, including twin brothers, Ardis and Wallace Russell.

With our modern, mobile society, it is becoming increasingly rare that people have the blessing of spending an entire childhood in one location. Yazoo City has always been the center of my universe. I have traveled far from home as an adult, perhaps making up for lost miles in my early years. Although my physical body has moved to Kentucky, Wisconsin, Georgia, and now California, my heart and mind have never been far from Graball Hill and the wonderful people of Yazoo City whose shared experiences were such a blessing to the Jenkins family.

CHAPTER 10

Yazoo International Airport

"Only two things are infinite, the universe and human stupidity, and I'm not sure about the former."
Albert Einstein (1879-1955)

The last thing I want is someone chronicling all the stupid things I've done. I've made enough mistakes to fill volumes. Since I try to live by the Golden Rule, I hesitate to point out the mistakes of others. However, there are exceptional mistakes made that merit retelling, lest they be forgotten. I try to learn from the mistakes of others, because I cannot possibly live long enough to make them all myself. So I'm not poking fun at an anonymous airline pilot, I am giving him the notoriety he rightly deserves for changing Yazoo City's airport into Yazoo International Airport.

Mahatma Gandhi said, "Freedom is not worth having if it does not include the freedom to make mistakes." I knew there was something in Gandhi's teachings to which I could relate.

I remember the day as if it was last week. The sun was shining, and we were busy about our chores. Mother had washed the clothes in the old scrub board tub, and hung them out to dry on the clothesline that ran behind the house toward the cistern. Topey and I were trying to play checkers between assignments to bring in some water or stove wood. The hogs had been slopped, the cows fed, weeds had been hoed out of the corn and bean gardens. I think Topey was winning. It was hard to tell since neither of us really knew the game rules and many of the pieces were missing. Eventually he lost interest after he ate the graham cracker we were using for one of the pieces, so he set off to visit Poochie Calhoun on the other side of Graball Hill. It did not bother me that my failings at checkers would be the subject of the two dogs' conversation. I pumped a bucket of water for a cool drink, and settled back for a rest near the barn. Just before my afternoon siesta, I thought how lucky I was to be living on Graball Hill.

At about this time, a major Southern airline, which shall not be specifically named for fear of legal repercussions, was ready for boarding at Memphis Airport. For the purposes of recounting this piece of history, it will be referred to herein as Kudzu Airlines. About half of the 76 seats were empty for the 11:20 a.m. departure to Jackson, Mississippi. Unlike the Yazoo City Airport, which was a tiny runway primarily used for crop dusting planes, the airport at Jackson, 40 miles away, was a fairly large and modern airport that accommodated the big aircraft of that day.

I never did know the name of the Captain and co-pilot on that particular flight, but in memory of their anonymity, will refer to them as Captains Mayday and Wrongway. No one knows for sure what happened. Sure, it was reported in the newspapers, but there was a lot of speculation among experts and laypersons as to the real story. *The New York Times* even reported the story, but made Yazoo City sound like a flea on a hound.

Captain Mayday conceivably could have nodded off or become confused because the flat Delta terrain was monotonous at best. It was a short 55 minute flight to Jackson. In Mississippi, the weather can change rather quickly. Dark clouds from the west could have reduced visibility. Nevertheless, on that fateful day, the Captain radioed Jackson Airport that he would make a visual approach, using the runway lights as his guide. Jackson replied in the affirmative.

What Captain Mayday did not know was Mississippi Chemical Corporation, a large fertilizer manufacturer in Yazoo City, had recently installed lights on top of their smoke stacks, ironically, to keep low flying crop dusting planes from crashing into them. "I see the lights," the Captain radioed to the Jackson Tower. "Roger," was Jackson Tower's reply.

It was not until the airplane broke below the cloud ceiling that Captain Mayday realized something was not right. Something was very, very wrong. He circled the plane twice right over our house.

The noise of the plane woke me from my siesta out by the barn. I didn't know what was happening! The first thing I heard was a loud roaring and the ground began to shake. Rev. Goodbody's Sunday sermon on Revelation and the end of the world kept flashing through my mind: "*Then I saw another beast come up out of the earth,*" Rev. Goodbody had read from the Bible. I took off running toward the house screaming for Momma as the noise and the earthshaking increased. "*The beast performed great signs, even making fire come down from heaven to earth in the sight of everyone*!"

"Please God," I prayed, "don't take me now! I ain't even ever kissed a girl yet!" Just then a dark cloud blocked out the sun. I was running as fast as I could but tears clouded my eyes. I tripped over a hoe and fell, face up, curled in a fetal position. Through my tears I could see the biggest airplane I had ever laid eyes on just a few dozen yards above my head. As scared as I was, I don't think there was as much anxiety in my face as there was in the passengers' faces I could see pressed against the windows above me. Some seemed to be saying to themselves, "This doesn't look like Jackson." Others, were probably saying, "What's wrong with that crazy boy down there?"

By the time Captain Mayday realized his terrible mistake, it was too late to pull up and make it on to Jackson. Luckily, Yazoo City Field was straight ahead. Unfortunately, our 500 foot airstrip was way too short for a big aircraft; but God loves Yazoo City and just beyond the runway was Mr. Kern's cotton field.

What Captain Mayday lacked in navigational acumen, he made up for in landing skills. Captains Mayday and Wrongway deserve credit for taking advantage of every inch of Yazoo City's runway. As the plane landed, a voice came over the loudspeaker: "Whoa, big fella. WHOA!" The giant plane skidded off the end of the airstrip into the soft Delta mud. Mr. Kern only lost two acres of cotton during the remainder of the landing, but no one was injured. It was an amazing sight, this metal behemoth rising above the white cotton patch. Immediately the doors popped open and inflatable slides came out from the doors. Bewildered people began sliding down into the cotton and circling around the plane. After a few stunned moments of silence, a white haired grandmother asked a young man next to her, "Sonny, did we land or were we shot down?" One of the flight attendants said "Sorry folks, for the rough landing. It wasn't the pilot's fault, and it wasn't the plane's fault. It was the lack of asphalt."

Kudzu Airlines dispatched a Greyhound bus to Yazoo City, and two hours later the somewhat shell-shocked passengers arrived in Jackson for the continuation of their trips.

That was the day I learned two great religious truths: first, you could find religion in a cotton field; and secondly, everybody wants to go to heaven, but nobody wants to die.

And as for the plane, it was impossible to fly it out of there because there was no suitable runway for a takeoff. That Kudzu Airline plane had to be taken apart, piece by piece, loaded on a flatbed truck and shipped to Jackson, where it was reassembled and put back into service.

CHAPTER 11

Main Street Memories

"When I was younger, I could remember anything, whether it had happened or not."
Mark Twain (1835-1910)

Main Street in Yazoo City holds many memories for me. I thank God for those recollections, and for a mind that can still call up precious images and events on a moment's notice. When I was younger, I was amused that old men could remember in great detail events from their childhood, but could not remember to zip up their fly when exiting the men's room. Now, as my memory takes me back down Main Street, I qualify as being old, and I keep checking to ensure my fly is closed.

Memory is a wonderful thing. It allows us to conjure up those perfect days of youth regardless of how imperfect today may be going. Any day in my mind can be September 20 in Yazoo City, when the first cold front of autumn pushes the long, hot summer into the Gulf of Mexico. Memory allows me to transcend the miles and the years, and reconstruct the games I played with my childhood friends, or relive the adolescent experiences my classmates and I shared. Mark Van Doren said, "*Memory performs the impossible for man; holds together past and present, gives continuity and dignity to human life.*"

Main Street stands divided North and South, with Broadway being the dividing line. Indeed, the intersection of Main and Broadway was the busiest in town. Main Street also stands divided in my memory between my childhood and teen years. The two-story buildings on South Main Street have survived for over a century. In some ways, they remain as they were; but they are constantly changing as they age, and as their role in commerce and culture change.

When I was a child in the 1950s, Main Street was where we went on Saturdays. If we completed our chores, and if we had been good, we received a dime for the Saturday afternoon matinee at one of Yazoo City's theaters; The Dixie or The Palace, and later, The Yazoo. We did not call them movies in those days; we called them picture shows. In the days before television, the picture shows were where we became fans of Roy Rogers and Gene Autry. Gene sang a little too much for my cowboy tastes, and I was a bit uncomfortable when he made "goo-goo" eyes at the cowgirls. I now know that was because my hormones had not kicked in. and have since made my share of "goo-goo" eyes. I've loved women ever since I discovered I wasn't one of them. But my life of "libido loco" could be the subject of a whole other book I am praying never gets written.

Going to the picture show was the most popular form of entertainment in Yazoo City. The movies we saw shaped our lives and our understanding of the "outside world", and introduced us to foreign places far from Yazoo City. After westerns, the Tarzan movies were my favorites, and I confess I got my share of bruises and scrapes trying unsuccessfully to swing from one tree to another on a kudzu vine. Sometimes, we got to see how rich people lived in movies like "Some

Like It Hot" and "Sabrina". I saw exotic locales, like Asia and California in movies like "The Bridge on the River Kwai" and "Sunset Boulevard". On Saturday afternoons "Godzilla", "Rodan", or "Invasion of the Body Snatchers" scared us witless. After movies like that, I felt extremely blessed to be sharing a bedroom and bed with my older brothers because I would have been too scared to have slept alone. I remember in 1956 when we saw "The Ten Commandments" starring Charlton Heston. The movie was very long, and had an intermission, probably to give the projectionist time to reload the reels. T-Baby didn't know what an intermission was, figured the movie was over, and went home. When I saw T-Baby later, he said, "That movie didn't have a good ending." I guess he only saw five of the Ten Commandments. That may also explain some of his conduct.

After the matinee, we romped up and down South Main Street, doing what might best be called window-shopping. For four blocks, stores on both sides of Main Street beckoned us to come inside, and spend the quarter we were given as our allowance. We would stop at Carr's drug store and get a Coke float at the soda fountain. We would go upstairs at Kuhn's department store, and scope out the latest toys. We would carefully calculate how many quarters we would have to save to buy the new toy car, or the Roy Rogers six-shooter, just like the one we saw at the matinee. It was an early lesson in frugality, which rarely resulted in us saving up for the big toy. We most often spent the quarter on a little toy, a tiny plastic horse that kept our imaginations satisfied for a week of playtime. Sometimes I would ask Tommy and Louis to spend their quarters on a plastic Indian or outlaw, and we would have a set we could share in our play. This, like many early experiences, taught us prudence and teamwork.

Mother and Pop dropped us off at the theater after noon, and went about their routine, their only respite from us in their demanding week. As long as we stayed on Main Street, there was no concern anyone would harm us. Those were more innocent days, and my memory finds it increasingly appealing to recall that innocence. We encountered all our childhood friends from church and school, who were enjoying their Saturday afternoon escape, just as we were. The store clerks looked out for us, and if any child had a problem, there was a trusted adult always nearby. As darkness approached, somehow we managed to reunite with our parents, who arrived on Main Street for their weekly window-shopping custom. When the appliance store put a new fangled television in the storefront window, a crowd would gather to see the marvel of pictures being transmitted through the air. We would show our parents how we had spent our quarters. If it had been a good week, Pop might give us another dime, and we would race back to Kuhn's, Woolworth's or McCrorys to see what cheap toys were left. The stores closed at nine, and we made our way back to Graball Hill, crowded in the family car, proud owners of a new inventory of toys.

I am not sure when Saturday nights on Main Street ended. Was it the stores that changed, or was it our shopping habits, or did we change? Probably all three, but mostly we changed. When I was no longer a boy, I wasn't as interested in plastic cowboys. I wanted to hang out with my friends. I wanted to see and be seen, especially by the girls. So the Saturday night window-shopping was replaced by "dragging Main" on Friday nights. When my friends and I were old enough to get driver's licenses, and could borrow our parent's car, we became initiated into the first phase of pre-courtship, dragging Main. Main Street was then a two-way street. It was exactly like the scenes in "American Graffiti" with carloads of junior high and high school kids cruising up and down Main Street. We would get dressed up like we had a real date, polish our penny loafers, and slap on some

"English Leather" cologne that was popular at the time. We boys would try to comb our hair into some semblance of a ducktail like Elvis Presley. Brylcreem advertised that "a little dab will do you" but two tubes full didn't work on me. Hairstyling was exceedingly difficult, as my hair was naturally very curly and did not want to smooth out into a pompadour, and certainly would not stand up in a crew cut either. I cursed that wavy hair back then, but now that my hair can't decide whether to turn gray or turn loose, that thick, wavy hair is another of my fond memories of youth.

Everyone else in town stayed away from Main on Friday nights, because of the constant stream of traffic traveling at 15 miles per hour. That was the only time we drove that slow, because we wanted to see who was in which car with whom, and we didn't want anyone to miss the opportunity to check us out. After as many passes down the street as we thought were effective, we would cruise over to the drive-in, ostensibly for cokes and snacks, but really hoping to meet up with some of the girls that we had given the eye on our earlier dragging.

Dragging Main was not limited to Main Street, but extended out Grand Avenue to the Tastee Freeze, the Teen Center on Jackson Avenue, and Fifteenth Street. Most of us were forbidden from getting on the highway. I will never forget the night we were cruising in Bobby David's new Corvair, a Chevy product with the engine in the rear, like a Volkswagen. We drove down Fifteenth and across the railroad tracks, not particularly fast, when we heard a thud and felt an awful scraping. Bobby David coasted the car to the side of the street, and when we looked back to see what happened, there was the whole dang engine sitting in the middle of Fifteenth! I still don't understand how that was possible, but I can still hear Bobby David calling his mother to come get us, and "Oh, by the way, the car engine fell out." My biggest concern was that no girls witnessed our humiliating experience.

I played trombone in the high school band. When we had home football games, and especially when we had homecoming, the city blocked off Main Street all the way from its starting point at Canal Street to the foot of Main near the banks of the Yazoo River, where the city fathers erected a giant plywood Santa Clause every Christmas. The band and majorettes marched the full distance of Main Street to the likes of "On Wisconsin" and "Red River Rock", followed by the football team and coaches, the cheerleaders, and the homecoming court in shiny new cars donated by the local auto dealers for the occasion. Merchants, parents, sports boosters, and shoppers lined the street, caught up in the magic of the moment.

As the years roll by, I sometimes march down Main Street again in my memories. There is hardly a building or an intersection that does not bring back memories of those Fridays and Saturdays, watching the matinees, window-shopping, and dragging Main. I see again the friends, places and the events that shaped my early life. Alexander Smith said, "*A man's real possession is his memory. In nothing else is he rich, in nothing else is he poor.*" As long as I have my memories of Main Street and Graball Hill, I will always have another quarter to spend before the stores close at nine.

CHAPTER 12

A Bum Breaks Up Church

"The greatest man in history was the poorest."
Ralph Waldo Emerson

Many of my childhood experiences revolved around church and music. Not only did my parents want us to get a good education, they wanted us to get a good sense of values. Don't get me wrong, no one is claiming moral perfection here. I've made enough mistakes for three lifetimes; but at least I know they were mistakes.

My parents did not subscribe to the notion of allowing us to grow up and choose which, if any, religion we wanted to select, any more than allowing us to grow up before deciding if we wanted to take baths, brush our teeth, go to school, do our chores and finish our homework. Today, I realize that having a firm faith foundation is about as important as anything a child can get. Too bad some modern parents don't see it that way. If parents are fearful of damaging their children by giving them religion, just think how damaged they will be for not having it. So church attendance, thank God, was not an option.

In order to join the Assured Brethren Church, you first had to pass a physical just to persevere through the schedule. Sunday school and morning worship was followed by training and evening worship. It was not unusual for us to be in church six hours or more each Sunday. I never understood why I was so tired after the Sabbath day of rest. Then there were midweek prayer meetings, church outreach, choir practice, mission groups, and weekday boys and girls clubs. Bobby David once said, "Sunday school starts at 9:00 a.m. Sunday, and gets out about...Tuesday."

My family all loved music, and it became a core value in our family. It was not only religious music. In his younger days, Pop played a fiddle in a country band in some pretty rough roadhouses. We never got the details of what became of his budding music career, but the last time Pop saw his fiddle, it was being smashed over some drunk's head in a backwoods honky tonk late one Saturday night in 1924. I think Pop thought wistfully of that fiddle often; especially when he watched Lawrence Welk on television. We inherited Pop's love for music. Marietta plays the piano, I worked my way through college on a band scholarship playing the trombone, and all of us sang.

Pop loved going to Gospel Singing conventions at the Jackson Municipal Auditorium, where we listened to the Blackwood Brothers, Statesmen, and Stamps quartets. We spent many Sunday afternoons in hot churches or ceiling fan-cooled courthouses where gospel singers gathered, taking turns leading their favorite hymns from the Stamps Baxter songbook. That was in addition to the demanding church schedule at Assured Brethren Church.

Pop also loved the ancient Sacred Harp music. This eerie music, sung in four-part harmony, was written with shaped notes and required no musical accompaniment in a minor key. "I'm Just a Poor Wayfaring Stranger" and even "Amazing Grace" had Sacred Harp origins. To the uninitiated, the haunting sound of Sacred Harp may be mistaken for the calls of a flock of geese flying south for the winter. I had an ear trained from childhood to appreciate the subtle beauty of this music form. The 2003 movie, "Cold Mountain," featured Sacred Harp music sung by Nicole Kidman. Among my fondest childhood memories are the annual May pilgrimages to Concord Baptist Church in Calhoun County for an all day Sacred Harp singing, where we visited the graves of our ancestors, and ate some of the best fried chicken and fried apple pies this side of heaven. My genuine enjoyment of those trips may have been what earned me the otherwise unwarranted title of Pop's favorite and the disdain of my older siblings.

Assured Brethren Church was located near the railroad tracks in Yazoo City. Occasionally, we would have a hobo pass by along the railroad tracks, visible through the open church windows. There was no air conditioning back then. Watching the hobos provided momentary distraction from Rev. Goodbody's sermon. Once, we even had a hobo wait outside the church until services were over. He asked for food. Food was never scarce at church, and the ladies located some cold biscuits and jelly left over from the men's breakfast that day. The hobo gulped them down with a mayonnaise jar of water before setting off again on his rambling journey. As long as the hobos kept their distance, and didn't disturb worship, we kept a peaceful coexistence with them.

On one particularly bright Sunday, we arrived at church for our weekly infusion of Bible study, singing, sermonizing, and fellowship. About halfway through the sermon, we heard the church door open. At first, I thought it was Topey coming in from making a necessary stop at the fire hydrant outside the church. Then, I heard whispered voices. Boy, someone was going to get a whipping when they got home, because one thing you never did is talk during the sermon. I turned to see who had experienced this lapse in moral turpitude. My eyes became as big as saucers. It was a hobo, a bum, who had the audacity to come into our church.

Aunt Minnie began fanning herself faster and faster with her Stricklin-King Funeral Home fan as the bum worked his way up the aisle, stopping to ask a question to the startled worshippers who had the misfortune of being seated next to the aisle. "Wilburn! Do something, quickly! Wilburn!" she said, reminiscent of the day Shugga and Topey used her middle section as a speedway. Rev. Goodbody tried to continue the sermon, but realized he had lost the attention of everyone to the stranger. The ushers composed themselves in time to grab the hobo and began escorting him out of God's house.

"The nerve of some people!" one particular Assured member said out loud.

"Wait a minute," Rev. Goodbody said to the ushers. "Bring that man down here."

The ushers turned and walked the bum to the front of the church, right in front of the pulpit. His clothes were relatively clean but very shabby. He looked like he hadn't shaved in two weeks. "Sir, in all my years in the ministry, I have never seen such a display of rudeness," the pastor said. "Don't you know I can call the Yazoo County sheriff and have you thrown in jail for disturbing a service of public worship?"

"I don't mean no harm," the hobo said apologetically, holding his tattered hat in his hands. "It's just that..." Rev. Goodbody interrupted, "Yes, we know, you just wanted some food, but you couldn't wait outside until we were finished. You had to come in here and ruin our service."

"No sir, that ain't why I come in here. I et a good breakfast of bacon and coffee this mornin'," the hobo said, managing a small smile for the good fortune of a meal.

Rev. Goodbody quickly responded, "Oh, so you want

money. I should have guessed. We just took up the offering, and you thought you were going to get a share of it?"

"No sir, that ain't it neither. You see, I hain't been feeling too good lately. I run into a doctor man who looked me over and told me I have somethin' pretty bad. He said I don't got much time left. I saw yore church sign, and read where it said, 'Looking for the Lord? Inquire within.' So, I just thought I needed to find the Lord, and that's what I been asking your good members. Can anyone tell me where to find the Lord?"

Silence, followed by more deafening silence. Then tears, hot burning tears running down the faces of everyone present. Then there came the shame for our quick judgment of the man.

Rev. Goodbody broke the silence. "Sir, I am sorry for misjudging you. I think I can tell you where to find the Lord." He stepped down from the pulpit; put his arm around the poor man, and the two men talked in soft tones. I couldn't understand what they said, but Aunt Minnie began singing, and others joined in.

"Softly and tenderly, Jesus is calling.
Calling for you and for me.
See on the portals, he's waiting and watching.
Watching for you and for me.
Come home, Come home.
You, who are weary, come home.
Softly and tenderly, Jesus is calling.
Calling for you and for me."
(Softly and Tenderly, by Will L. Thompson)

After Rev. Goodbody and the hobo prayed quietly together, the Reverend said, "I think God sent a different sermon this morning than the one I prepared."

Over the years, I have often recalled the day the bum

broke up church. It needed breaking up, and so did our stony, Assured hearts. Sometimes, I wish he would show up at my church, and remind me and the whole congregation that pointing people to the Lord is much more important than making it through the service without interruption.

> "*Then the righteous will answer him, 'Lord, when did we see you hungry and feed you, or thirsty and give you something to drink? When did we see you a stranger and invite you in, or needing clothes and clothe you? When did we see you sick or in prison and go to visit you?' The King will reply, 'I tell you the truth, whatever you did for one of the least of these brothers of mine, you did for me.'*" (Matthew 25:37-40)

CHAPTER 13

A Pinch of Religion

"If you cannot get rid of the family skeleton, you may as well make it dance."
George Bernard Shaw (1856-1950)

Southerners take their religion, politics, football, and coffee strong. One day an Assured Brethren woman came upon a man standing on the edge of the Yazoo River Bridge. "Why are you standing there?" she asked. "I have lost all hope, and I am going to jump to my death," he replied. "Wait, let's talk. Are you a Christian?" "Yes," the despondent man replied. "Me, too. Are you Protestant?" The man said he was Protestant. "Me too. Are you an Assured Brethren?" "As a matter of fact, I was reared Assured Brethren," the man replied. "See, we have a lot in common. Are you Nashville Synod?" The depressed man seemed to forget his troubles. "As a matter of fact I am." "King James Version (KJV) or New American?" The man responded, "I'm New American!" "Jump, you heretic, jump!" the woman said.

Assured Brethren were evangelicals, meaning we were

on a mission to save the souls of everyone from damnation, especially souls across the oceans. That was an ambitious and noble calling. The church instilled in us a concern for the souls of our loved ones. Many of Rev. Goodbody's sermons included long passionate appeals for reprobates to come forward and repent of their sins. With "every head bowed, and every eye closed," I sometimes sneaked a peek to see if I could pick out the reprobates in the congregation. Rev. Goodbody must have known something I didn't, because it looked like everyone present was a bona fide ABC, Nashville Synod, and KJV. Maybe the pastor wasn't sure all of ours were going to make it to heaven? But if being ABC-NS-KJV wasn't enough to get you to heaven, then who could possibly be saved? Topey and I held many theological discussions on the subject.

I have always subscribed to the notion that sermons should be like women's skirts; short enough to attract interest, but long enough to cover the subject. Mini skirts and mini sermons were unheard of in our church. Rev. Goodbody certainly wasn't known for brief sermons. I could tell the parson was in trouble when Aunt Minnie started squirming in her pew. After the extended invitation, I overheard her whisper to Uncle Wilburn, "When is that preacher going to learn that the mind cannot absorb any more than the behind can endure?"

In those days, no businesses in the Deep South operated on Sundays, except hospitals, the fire departments, and some restaurants. As the clock ticked closer to noon, I thought, "Darn, the Methodists are going to beat us to Danries Restaurant again for lunch." I hated it when the Methodist girls would stick their tongues out at us when we were the last in line for the blue-plate special, fried catfish and okra. "Look, the ABCs are XYZ again," they said. I stuck my tongue out back at them, but harbored secret fantasies of becoming a Methodist, for both the shorter sermons and the pretty girls.

Our patience was rewarded when someone actually acknowledged being a reprobate, and responded to Rev. Goodbody's invitation. I recall an unusually good season for the pastor, when he had a half dozen converts in a span of a few weeks. A couple of the converts were actually repeat offenders, but we were more than happy to re-baptize them if the first dunking didn't take. Besides, it made the number of converts we reported to Nashville look more impressive, even if half of them were recycled. The pastor scheduled a baptism service for the fourth Sunday in May. Being Assured Brethren, the converts had the option of being immersed, poured, or sprinkled. Almost everyone elected to be immersed. We didn't want the Baptists calling us "shallow water" Christians.

The fourth Sunday arrived, and we gathered on the banks of the Yazoo River at the foot of South Main. The first to be baptized was Mr. Clay, a local merchant. He was a handsome man with a nice head of hair for his age. We were particularly pleased to have leaders of the business community as members, and hoped he tithed. Next was Mrs. Clay, the merchant's wife, a rather large woman. Rev. Goodbody pronounced the appropriate words and proceeded to push Mrs. Clay back into the muddy Yazoo, but her feet popped up. Realizing it wasn't an official Assured Brethren baptism unless he got all of her under water at the same time, he pushed down on her feet, but her head popped back up. Rev. Goodbody called for the deacons to help. It took three men to get Mrs. Clay virtuously baptized. By the time the last convert stood before Rev. Goodbody, he was glad the service was coming to a close. Suddenly, he noticed a furry object floating toward him. What else could go wrong? Should he ignore it? It seemed to swim faster and faster toward the pastor. He reached out and grabbed the hairy beast, thinking it may have been a rabid beaver. When he opened his hand, he saw it was a man's toupee. That's when he noticed the drenched and embarrassed Mr. Clay standing on the banks of the Yazoo, bald as an eagle. Coincidentally, that is also when new converts began opting to be poured or sprinkled rather than immersed.

Revival time came around each year in August, when the crops were "laid by," meaning the farmers had done all the cultivating they could do. The only thing left was to pray for rain and await the harvest. Since there was less work in the fields, it was a good time to hold protracted religious services. I can remember revivals that went on for two weeks. We went to church twice on Sunday and every night of the week, including Saturdays, during revival. Usually, a guest preacher came in to conduct the meetings, one with strong evangelistic skills. Whether it was because of the fervent prayers, or just sheer exhaustion, many decisions were recorded during revival. We were encouraged to bring our friends and neighbors, especially the reprobates, and even the Methodists and Baptists, because we were not completely assured they were brethren. Members who brought visitors—prospects we called them—received special recognition.

I was pretty sure all my family was assured. Topey was for sure, but probably not Shugga. I had written her off as a wayward soul. The only person the Lord "laid on my heart" was T-Baby Calhoun. If there ever was anyone on Graball Hill or in Yazoo County, who needed assurance, it was T-Baby. But if I invited T-Baby to church, he would only laugh at me, and then whip my tail. I had heard the stories of how our ABC missionaries suffered greatly for the gospel. I was ashamed that I was not willing to suffer for the cause. So I mustered my courage, enlisted Topey for moral support, and marched over to the other side of Graball Hill to the Calhoun's house. T-Baby spotted me coming up the trail. He met me at the gate, and said, "Hey Junior. Don't mess with me, I'm T-Baby Calhoun." "I know you can whip my tail, T-Baby. I didn't come to fight. I came to invite you to our revival." I said, ready to bolt if T-Baby made any move. "I ain't never been to church," he said. "Well, you ought to try it. You'll never know if you like it until you try it." "I'll think about it, Junior," T-Baby said. "Now get your sorry tail off my property."

I took satisfaction in the knowledge I had invited the notorious T-Baby Calhoun to church. Getting T-Baby baptized would be as big as converting the Pope. But I was convinced T-Baby would never darken the doors of our church.

That night, the church was full. The guest preacher and Rev. Goodbody had motivated the members to bring visitors to this special service. We sang and prayed and were having a wonderful time. I looked around, but T-Baby was nowhere to be found. That did not surprise me. Then, just as the guest preacher began his sermon, the door behind us opened, and in stepped T-Baby Calhoun. One of the ushers ran out of the church in fear for his life. I ran back into the vestibule, and greeted T-Baby. I proudly escorted him down the aisle to the last remaining seat, in the center of the first pew. If I had died at that moment, I'm sure Saint Peter would have personally opened the pearly gates for me, because I had snagged the biggest prospect in the whole county. I was sure this would be a source of great irritation to the Methodists and Baptists.

T-Baby sat down in the center of the pew, right where the two boards came together. On one side of him was my Aunt Minnie, and on the other side of him was Mrs. Clay. They were both large women, and had caused the boards that met right where T-Baby was sitting to spring open just a smidgen. As the preacher waxed eloquent, and landed a good blow to the Nashville Synod – New American heretics, both Aunt Minnie and Mrs. Clay jumped to their feet shouting "Amen, Amen, You tell 'em preacher, Amen."

There is a law of physics that says when you are sitting on the crack of a pew, and three hundred pounds on your left and three hundred pounds on your right suddenly leave the plane of the pew, move your tail quickly, or else it will be in a painful crack. T-Baby was never good at physics. "Aaaaaaawwwwwwwah," T-Baby cried, in agony that his tail was literally in a pinch. "Aaaaaawaaahh," he screamed again. Have you ever had a pain so sharp you couldn't talk? The church members rushed to T-Baby, certain he was having a spiritual experience. They began patting him on the back, saying, "Praise the Lord! Praise the Lord!" All T-Baby could say was another, "Aaaaawwwwah." Fortunately, Aunt Minnie and Mrs. Clay sat back down to console T-Baby in his moment of spiritual ecstasy. The law of physics worked in reverse, and T-Baby sprang free, knocking down two deacons as he flew out of the church, never to return.

I've often thought of that night and T-Baby's soul. Did he get religion? Is he assured? I will not know for sure until I get to heaven. I take small consolation that for all the pain T-Baby caused my rear end, his was in a crack the night he got a pinch of religion.

CHAPTER 14

Family of Cars

"If everything is under control, you are going too slow."
Mario Andretti (1940-)

When Daddy was born in 1901 in Calhoun County, he could not have imagined the automobile, or the influence those horseless carriages would have upon our family. I cannot say for sure when he saw his first car, but I am quite sure it was love at first sight. I know for sure he bought the first car he could scrape up the money for. I have a photo of my father, looking rather dapper in his 1930s outfit, standing next to his Model T. Our home may have looked like an abandoned sharecropper's shack, but all his life, my father had a fine automobile.

I have family photos that chronicle my growth. Most of them are taken outdoors, due to lack of flash equipment, and most have cars in the photo. Looking back, I am not sure if the photos are chronicling the Jenkins' kids or the Jenkins' cars. One is from 1955, where I am standing in front of our beloved, but dilapidated house. I hadn't noticed until recently, but behind me in that photo is Pop's brand new 1955

Cadillac. Another photo is dated 1957. There was the same old house, but with a shiny new 1957 Chevrolet parked out front. I do not need many more photos to validate the pattern, for by 1957, I knew whatever else might have happened, every year we got a brand new car. As poor as we were, how did we always manage to have a new car? It was a perk of Pop's job.

Pop Jenkins was a master car salesman, not only did he sell cars to parents and their children, he sold cars to their grandchildren as well. He worked at Valley Chevrolet in Yazoo City on Calhoun Avenue behind the new hospital. Yazooans trusted Pop, and every three years or so, they came to him to get their new set of wheels. One of the perks of being a salesman was getting a demonstrator car that Pop drove until it sold at a discount for being "slightly used." Everyone knew the demo cars were well cared for. Sometimes Pop would come home a bit dejected, because he was such a good salesman, he had sold his favorite demo. That only meant he got to order a new demo, and we hardly ever had a car that had lost the new car smell.

Norman and Tommy inherited our father's love for cars. One reason I think my brothers were so industrious was so they could buy their own cars. Norman's first car was a 1947 Chevy he bought with Pop's help. Maybe Pop was a bit possessive of his car, and wanted Norman to have a car of his own. Norman fixed that car up, sold it, and bought a 1941 Ford, an older but more sporty car, and began a series of upgrades that mirrored the car advancement program of our father. Tommy owned a new Corvette Sting Ray almost as soon as he could drive. Needless to say, he was popular in high school and that wasn't just because the car was a babe magnet. He was good looking and charming besides. Tommy loved drag racing, and won many trophies. He was constantly tinkering with the car, its engine, or some automotive accessory. Albert Einstein was a bookworm, but he had enough common sense to say, "*Any man who can drive safely while kissing a pretty girl is simply not giving the kiss the attention it deserves.*" But Einstein never met my brother, Tommy.

At times, we had two cars. I think Pop would pick up an old clunker, fix it, and sell it for a decent profit. I remember we took one of those cars to Kingsport, Tennessee to visit Momma and Daddy Roberts. That was a thirteen-hour drive, and Pop was not known for his bathroom stops. If there was gas in the tank, it was not time for a pit stop. My bladder was not cooperating with Pop's stop schedule, so he told me pick up the floor mat on the passenger side of the back seat. There I saw a hole in the floorboard, and the blur of asphalt rushing underneath. What did this have to do with my pressing need? "Make water," Pop said. The same man who wrote the woodpecker poem couldn't say "pee" in mixed company. Children should obey their parents, so I confess I took a whiz through the hole in the floorboard going sixty miles an hour. The only redeeming factor was at that time, three o'clock in the morning, all my siblings were asleep, except Louis who began calling me "Bullseye."

I can recall our Bel-Air that nearly spelled the end of Louis when he was four and I was six. We were living at the old house and all piled into Pop's new 1954 Chevy. We were on our way to church, but that didn't necessarily mean it was Sunday. There was something going on at our church at least five days a week. I think that Chevy could find the Assured Brethren Church even if Topey steered it. Anyway, with nine people crowded into one car, it's hard to keep count, and if one falls out, well, you still have eight left. Pop was impatient with us because we were running late. He led the singing to open the service, and hated to be late. Ellen, Norman, and Linda were already in the back and slammed the rear right side shut while Louis and I jumped into the left side of the back seat. Louis was next to the window and pulled the door, but didn't get it shut all the way. He leaned on the door to push it open in an attempt to pull it back shut. By now, the car was in motion. Louis tumbled out of the moving car, and I think he actually rolled under it. The Bel-Air ran over him, but did not touch him. I looked back through the rear window. Yep, that was my little brother lying on the ground between the tire ruts in the dirt driveway. "Hey, Pop," I said, "I think we lost one." Pop looked in his rear view mirror, and threw the car in reverse. He picked up a somewhat bewildered Louis, dusted him off, and sat him in the back seat before securely closing the door. Those were the days before child car seats, much less seat belts. Louis, stunned, was no worse for the ordeal. We all had reason to offer special thanks when we arrived at church.

What are little brothers for, if not to annoy you and to borrow money from? Being the least industrious of the four brothers, I decided the only way I would ever get a car was to go into a partnership with my little brother Louis. He agreed, and we each put up $25 and bought an old clunker for $50. I think it was a 1953 Studebaker. That year was 1965. In Southern parlance, the car had been "ridden hard, and put up wet." It leaked oil, and the transmission was shot. Twice in the first month, I had to call someone to come pick me up because the old car just up and died on me. At that time, neither Louis nor I were the mechanics Norman and Tommy were. They offered a bit of help, but their hormones were working just fine, and they had better things on their minds than fixing our rolling disaster looking for a place to happen. That place came a week later, when I was driving the car home from work. I made a left on Broadway precisely under the Main Street traffic light. In the immortal words of Author Unknown, my favorite sage, "I felt like I was diagonally parked in a parallel universe." Our '53 Studebaker died in the middle of the busiest intersection in Yazoo City, blocking traffic in all four directions. When the tow truck driver asked me where I wanted it delivered, I said the bottom of the Yazoo River sounded good to me, and as far as I know, that car is still down there.

My mechanical skills haven't improved a bit. I've joined the AAA, even though I don't drink, because they will come get me if my old Chevy van with 110,000 miles goes dead in the middle of San Diego's busiest intersection at rush hour. Call it insurance for "falling off the wagon".

My life's passion has been technology, not automobiles. Oh sure, I appreciate a beautiful car as much as I appreciate beautiful sunsets and beautiful women. At my age, I am having a difficult time remembering why I like looking at beautiful cars and beautiful women so much. My driving philosophy has been to never drive faster than my guardian angel can fly.

CHAPTER 15

Puppy Love

"Nothing takes the taste out of peanut butter quite like unrequited love."
Charles M. Schulz (1922-2000),
Charlie Brown in *"Peanuts"*

The late J. D. Sumner of the Stamps Quartet, who sang with Elvis Presley, once recorded that "puppy love is caused by a woman leading a man to a dog's life". I have a higher view of love, whether of the puppy or old dog variety. But I would be the first to agree that puppy love is best experienced in the early part of life. Don't get me wrong. I have nothing against love. I am the eternal optimist as well as the eternal romantic. Like measles, it's best to catch puppy love while you are young, and build up immunity for old age.

I don't remember formal sex education; although I am sure my parents and teachers felt they did their part. Growing up on the farm has its advantages, and you pick up subtle hints about the birds and bees and calves and piglets. But then I was ten years old before I figured out dogs were not the daddies and cats were not the mommies. Topey got a good laugh out of that one.

I remember chasing the girls during recess in elementary school. When I would catch one, I would say, "Give me a kiss and I'll let you go." (These were the days before you could get expelled for sexual harassment.) "Forget it, Bozo," was the usual reply, and I let the girl go before she slugged me. One day I caught a particularly slow-moving girl named Nancy. "Give me a kiss and I'll let you go," I said. "OK," she said, as she puckered up her lips. "Uh oh, what do I do now?" I said to myself. That's when I learned the excitement is in the chase. I also learned that the fastest women were not always the most affectionate. It takes a man a few years to learn that he chases a woman until she catches him.

I remember one day when the principal at our Junior High called all the boys into the gymnasium, and the girls went to the auditorium. I am sure they felt they were doing their job in giving us sex education, but they told us we would go blind if we did certain things—but didn't really explain what those things were. T-Baby seemed to know what they were talking about and said he was willing to risk one eye.

Most boys go through a phase just like Spanky in "Our Gang" who started the "He-man Woman Haters Club". It didn't take me long to realize I was more like Alfalfa, who sneaked away to see Darla when the guys were not looking.

Albert Einstein, that sex symbol of the 1940s, said, "Gravitation is not responsible for people falling in love." Albert knew a lot about physics and love. I had stepped in puppy love a couple of times before I fell into it hard at age ten. Call them false starts. That was the first time I remember being head over heels, crazy in love with a girl in my fourth grade class whom we shall call Darlene. Of course she was a blond with blue eyes, and prettier than a newborn piglet. We were both in Mrs. Shaw's homeroom at Annie Ellis Elementary. My grades took a nosedive, not that they were all that great to begin with, because I found myself stealing glances at Darlene more than listening to Mrs. Shaw. I wanted to be sure I memorized everything about her, because when I went home, I saw her face in all my chores. I could say I saw her face while cleaning out the barn, which was true, but that takes some of the luster off puppy love.

I was much too shy to tell Darlene how I felt about her, and much too unsophisticated to know what to do after that. There was the fear of rejection, as well as the fear of her saying, "Oh William, I was hoping you felt that way, too. I can't sleep at nights thinking about you. I'm so glad to know you love me as much as I love you". Would we get married right away? Would I drop out of fourth grade to get a job to support my wife? Would we start a family right away? And by the way, how do you start a family? And would Rev. Goodbody have time in his busy schedule to perform the ceremony?

Overcoming my fear of being banned from our version of the He-man Woman Hater's Club, I accidentally on purpose let it slip to my best friend Bobby David that I liked Darlene; liked her "a whole lot". Bobby David said something like, "Really?" but didn't understand his role in this soap opera was to tell Darlene so I could know once and for all if there was a future for us. After explaining to Bobby David that "You better NOT tell her" really meant, "You BETTER tell her," Bobby David got with the plan, and told Darlene that William Jenkins liked her. Like the true lady I will always remember Darlene to be, she said something like, "Really? That's nice," and continued with her game of hopscotch. She was not the last female to rip out my heart and stomp that sucker flat.

It took me three years to get over Darlene. The love bug bit again in the seventh grade, right on schedule with the hormones. I don't think Dr. Morehead, our family doctor, had a shot for love sickness. Our Junior High included the seventh and eighth grades at the new school on Webster Avenue. On cold mornings before school, we were allowed to congregate in the basketball gym. One day, she walked in and the whole place seemed to light up. She was a new girl in town, and maybe that was what caught my eye at first. I had known all the other girls for six years, or longer if they attended Assured Brethren Church. This was a woman of mystery, and she had curves. She had blue eyes, and I began to notice a pattern. She was a brunette. She wasn't in my homeroom. Seventh grade was when we began changing classrooms every hour. I waited for the bell to ring every hour of the day, and looked for her until I memorized her class schedule. I walked far out of my way so I could pass her in the hall, and smile at her. But alas, nothing grew from my eternal love for…whatever her name was. After about a week, I passed her walking to class with one of the football players, arm in arm, making "goo-goo" eyes at each other. She moved away before the end of the eighth grade. I sometimes imagined her walking into some gymnasium, maybe at Grenada High School, before the first bell, and wanted to warn the guys that she would only break their hearts. But what can you really tell a teenage boy about a pretty, mysterious woman when the hormones begin coursing through our veins?

In high school, I stayed pretty busy. I was in the marching, concert, and stage bands, on the debate team, in the drama club, and kept up my obligations at church. The fact that I was too shy to ask a girl out on a date was camouflaged by the activities, but girls were never far from my mind.

It must have been the tenth or eleventh grade. I had my driver's license, and all my buddies were getting steady girlfriends. Rather than going for the prettiest girls in school, I decided to take a different approach. I would ask a ninth grader out. Yeah, that's the plan. She would look up to me as an upperclassman. I would be like her big brother, and teach her things older men know. She would be so grateful, and her girlfriends would be so jealous. I took inventory of the ninth grade girls, somewhat like a lion singling out a weak zebra from the herd. Then I spotted her. Let's call her Mavis. She was cute and innocent. I found it amazingly easy to walk right up to her and start a conversation. It seemed to terrify her. I asked her if she had plans for Friday night and would she like to go out with me? Mavis responded, "Well, I guess so." She probably had hoped some guy would just walk up and ask her out, but I had the uneasy feeling I was not the guy she was anticipating. Anyway, my first real date was on, and if it turned out to be a disaster, so what!

My first date with Mavis was a nightmare. I picked her up at 7:00 in my mother's car, and her father said, "Now have her home by 10:00." I opened the car door for her like a gentleman. As we drove to Danries Restaurant, I could tell it was going to be a long night. "How was your day?" I asked. "Fine," Mavis responded nervously. I wasn't expecting a one-word response; I was expecting a conversation. As I learned that night, expectations and reality are often far apart. Two minutes later, I thought up another question. "Nice weather, isn't it?" "Yes," Mavis said. I nervously turned up the car radio to listen to "Night Train" on WAZF, and to fill the silence with music. We arrived at Danries, and ordered hamburgers, malts, and fries. Mine was good, and I gulped it down. Mavis fiddled with a few French fries, and said, "I guess I'm just not hungry." From where I was sitting, that seemed to be an accurate statement. She wasn't hungry; she was terrified. I tried not to take it personally. I had been uncomfortable around many people, mostly T-Baby. But this was the first time I was aware anyone was uncomfortable around me. Did she think I was an axe murderer? Did she think I was going to expect her to go to Four Points and make out before going home? Hey, I was president of the Young Adult Moral Society (YAMS for short), and I had a reputation to uphold.

After our hamburgers, I suggested we drag Main Street, and talk. We drug Main Street, but I would not say we talked. I finally ran out of questions to ask. There was one awkward moment I will never forget. After an eternity in which it was painfully obvious we had nothing in common and nothing to say to each other, we both started a sentence at the same time. "You go first." "No, you go first." "No you." "I forgot what I was going to say." "Oh, me too." At least that was the longest conversation we had all evening. I got Mavis home well before her curfew, at 7:53 p.m. It may be the world's record for the shortest date in history.

Having suffered the third strike in puppy love, I went to T-Baby, who didn't seem to have the kind of problems I was having with the ladies. I knew T-Baby was very familiar with the goings-on at Four Points—things guys like me only heard rumors about. T-Baby was ruggedly handsome, in a James Dean sort of way, and had that "bad boy" thing going for him that seemed to attract certain girls. T-Baby called them "fast women," but I thought that was because they went with guys who drove fast cars. T-Baby picked up his guitar, and in his best Elvis impression began singing, "*And they call it puppy love*." I thanked T-Baby for his advice, although I found it no more helpful than the sex education day in the Junior High gym.

This is the sad story of my failed early attempts at puppy love. I am pleased to report my romantic life did not end there. I have come to understand that puppy love is one of those tricks life plays on us to get us ready for something wonderful, or else we would not recognize it when the real thing comes along, and we get to hunt the foxes with the big dogs.

CHAPTER 16

Yazoo, Yazoo, We Are So Proud Of You!

"I have never let my schooling interfere with my education."
Mark Twain (1835-1910)

Stanley C. Beers, our band director, wrote our high school song, "Yazoo, Yazoo" It still brings tears to my eyes, as do many of my high school experiences. Some of those experiences were sentimental and nostalgic, and some were outright embarrassing.

"Yazoo, Yazoo,
We are so proud of you!
And proud we'll always be
When we hear thy name."

"Yazoo, Yazoo,
We are so proud of you,
And forever and a day
We'll be thinking of you.
Yazoo, Yazoo."

Our high school, which included grades nine through twelve, was located at the corner of Canal and College where Grand Avenue began. The building is still there, but it is no longer used as the high school. If those walls could only talk, what stories they could tell! Many of us are glad the walls are mute, but it's fun to conjure up some of those memories.

It was the era of Frankie Avalon and Annette Funicello. We tried to dress like them and act like them. The girls wore puffed up hairdos, especially one called the beehive. Mini skirts were still a couple years away, darn the luck, but hemlines were above the knees and rising. Jumpers and pleated skirts and sweaters were popular with the girls. Both the girls and boys wore plaid; all kinds of plaid. When you look back at our Mingo Chito school annual you would have thought Yazoo City High had a school uniform of plaid shirts and blouses and tan pants and skirts. The guys wore long hair, and carried combs to slick their hair back in duck-tails. We were sometimes allowed to wear dark pants and white T-shirts, especially when it was hot, and fancied ourselves to look like Elvis or James Dean.

My guess is there were about 600 students in the four grades. My 1966 graduating class had 166 members. The school had adequate, but well-worn facilities located on two floors, including a nice auditorium, where we conducted school assemblies and formal occasions, such as the senior play, where I played the role of Guy Hawkins, a 21-year old first grader and bully in Jesse Stuart's autobiographical "The Thread That Runs So True". In dress rehearsal, Wesley Coleman, who played the role of Jesse Stuart, a first year schoolteacher, and I got into a staged fight. Wesley accidentally pushed me into a chair, and I almost missed opening night due to a pulled muscle in my back. But alas, I toughed it out and the show went on. Once, the school invited Miss Eudora Welty from Jackson to our assembly. Miss Welty read to us from her famous writings, an honor we did not fully recognize at the time.

We had a cafeteria, gymnasium, band room, and even a bomb shelter. Those were the days of the Cold War, and we lived in fear that an atomic explosion would wipe out Yazoo City. I was convinced that somewhere in the USSR, some Communist General had a map of the USA, and was pressing a pin into Yazoo City saying, "Boris, let's bomb here first." We received specific instructions on what to do when the blast occurred, and had drills on how we should instinctively drop below our desks when we heard the explosion and saw the flash of light. T-Baby would hit the floor every time a passing car backfired. I never really understood how my little wooden desk was going to protect me from a 10,000 pound atomic bomb. What we never learned was who would be allowed to enter the bomb shelter, a metal structure about 12 by 15 feet. I guess that was reserved for a few survivors who would have the responsibility of repopulating the world after the atomic war. I was willing to volunteer for the duty, and even had a couple of girls in mind as good candidates for my mate. The school kept the bomb shelter stocked with water and non-perishable food. The fact that it was there, behind the school next to the industrial arts shop offered some comfort in those days of uncertainty.

I did not appreciate it then, but our teachers were among the finest in America. We thought they were just plain mean, because they expected us to study, work, learn, and become productive citizens. I called my teachers the Four Horsemen of the Apocalypse (Famine, Pestilence, War and Death). Mrs. Parker (Death), the English teacher, was especially notorious for assigning two hours worth of homework each night. I saw my older siblings struggle to do all she expected, even spending their weekends trying to get all the work done, and knew my time was coming. No one got through Yazoo City High without spending at least one year in Mrs. Parker's English class. I thought at the time such work was cruel, unusual and inhumane treatment. Mrs. Parker taught some of my classmates' parents, and didn't have a gray hair in her unusually black hair (this added to her "Death" title). When she attended our thirtieth high school reunion, I was glad to see she finally allowed the gray hairs to crown her head with a beauty worthy of such an elegant lady.

One day, T-Baby showed up in Mrs. Parker's class without his homework assignment completed. "T-Baby, you are not going to tell me Poochie ate your homework again, are you?" "No ma'am," he replied, "Honest, I did it all last night. I don't know what happened. Maybe it is having an out of notebook experience."

Mrs. Parker was particularly proud of her prize student, Willie Morris, and rightly so. Willie graduated before I reached high school. He was editor of the school newspaper, "The Flashlight," which won national awards and served as the springboard for Willie's journalistic and writing career. "The Flashlight" later became known as "The Yazooan," but for years to follow its staff operated under the high standards and expectations set by Willie Morris and Mrs. Parker.

Then there was the Chieftan, the school bus. For at least a couple decades, the Chieftan took athletic teams, the band, cheerleaders, and participants in a host of school events on memorable trips. For many, those were our first trips outside Yazoo County. Many of us experienced our first kiss on the Chieftan, thanks to nighttime drives home from Big 8 events. Not even the chaperone can see in the dark, especially if you and your girlfriend sit on the back seat of the bus and pretend you are asleep. By the time I entered high school, the Chieftan was on its third engine, and commonly broke down on trips to Vicksburg, Biloxi and Jackson. In 1966, we retired the old Chieftan, but the famous old school bus still rides in my memories.

I played trombone in the high school band. We held pep rallies in the auditorium on football game days. The band sat on risers, saxophones on the lower level, trumpets on the first riser, and trombones on the second riser, about five feet above the stage floor. We played fight songs between the cheerleader's routines. The school's favorite band tune was "Red River Rock" because it had a rock and roll beat to it, unlike most of the John Phillip Sousa marches we played. Some students would stand in the aisle and do the "Twist" as we played. The trombones had a nice solo in that popular song. My friend Jimmy, who also played trombone, scooted his chair back in anticipation of the moment when we would "blow our own horns". I leaned over and told Jimmy to be careful, because we were on the edge of the highest riser. He kept scooting his chair further back, wanting all the room possible for our trombone slides to operate. Just as the trombone solo started, Jimmy's chair flipped backwards off the riser. His fall was broken when the top of his chair hit the wall just behind us. Jimmy was suspended in mid air in his chair at a 45-degree angle, wedged between the wall and the riser where the front two legs of his chair appeared to be holding on for dear life. I wasn't sure if I should stop playing and help him back on the riser, or play the trombone solo that had now arrived. Being the only trombonist left, I elected to keep playing, while the student body roared with laughter at Jimmy's precarious situation. Jimmy leaned forward and grabbed the right rear leg of my chair in an attempt to pull himself up, but only succeeded in pulling my chair dangerously close to the edge of the riser. The laughter got louder, and Mr. Beers speeded up the already hopping "Red River Rock". As soon as the trombone solo was over, I helped Jimmy to his full and upright position, amid the cheers and laughs of our classmates. From then on, Jimmy and I wore the nicknames, "Batman and Robin" for our agility and ability to scale walls before an audience of 600 classmates.

I wish to say I have no idea how Coach Rush's Volkswagen bug wound up on top of the high school roof. My name was associated with that prank, but I wish to take advantage of this opportunity to clear my name and restore my reputation. It took a crane brought in from Jackson to get the tiny car off the roof. How it got up there, and who put it there, remains a mystery, but I will always suspect that T-Baby had something to do with it.

Mr. Massey, our world history teacher, was a tall, thin, gentle person with large eyebrows and thick-rimmed glasses. I remember how Mr. Massey's multiple choice questions spelled out words so he could more easily grade papers. If we could get a few letters in place and could figure out the rest of the word, we got all the multiple choice questions right, whether we knew the correct answer or not. I think of it as an early form of "Wheel of Fortune". He never figured out we cracked his code. Despite his easy tests, he was a great teacher.

One day, T-Baby showed up late for Mr. Massey's final exam. It didn't really matter, T-Baby wasn't prepared. To his great surprise and delight, T-baby found the entire test was True/False. He pulled out a nickel, and began flipping the coin, marking True for heads and False for tails. After every other student left, Mr. Massey asked T-Baby why he was still flipping his coin. "I'm checking my answers," T-Baby replied.

Miss Touchstone was unmarried, and took world trips in the summer. Once she brought some chocolate covered ants from India, and ate them in front of us. Like they say, protein is protein. Miss Touchstone reminded me of Eudora Welty in appearance, and I loved her dearly. She taught American and Mississippi history as well as government, my favorite subjects. She knew her stuff, and inspired me to learn more.

Probably the teacher I owe the most to is Harriett DeCell. Her husband, Herman DeCell, was an Ivy League educated lawyer and state senator representing Yazoo County. Mrs. DeCell sponsored the debate team I was on. We spent many long hours after school and on weekends going over and over our debate strategy, proving our points and finding flaws in the logic of our opposition. She made us feel like we were lawyers, preparing the most important case we would ever argue. She showed me how to make a matrix of all possible arguments, and to have my response ready in advance. She tolerated no surprises, and no laziness. I have four superior debate certificates in my high school memento box , thanks to Mrs. DeCell, who taught me how to study, prepare and deliver my arguments on my feet and under pressure. Alas, my excellence in debating has not served me well in marital discussions, and has probably caused me to sleep on the couch on more than one occasion.

One Friday, Rev. Goodbody was asked to make a special presentation on the effects of alcohol on the human body before the entire student assembly. Gladly accepting this opportunity to uphold the moral standards for Yazoo City's youth, Rev. Goodbody poured a glass of whiskey and held a couple of earthworms over the glass, then dropped them in. The worms wriggled in anguish, and soon died. "So what does this mean to a person who puts alcohol in his or her stomach?" the Reverend said empathically. "I know," said T-Baby, "it means they won't have worms."

I remember the touch football games we played after lunch, the fun of hanging out with friends as we waited for the first bell in the morning, and the freedom to go home or to Mr. Alias' store for lunch if we didn't want to eat the "mystery meat special" offered in the cafeteria. I remember T-Baby's occasional explosions in the chemistry lab, (he wasn't much good with chemistry, either), and how hard it was to stay awake during fifth period on warm afternoons. I remember passing notes in the library, and the election where Halcy Barbour was elected president of the Student

Council, a premonition of things to come, as he is now governor. I remember John and Paul Evans, brothers who were treasured friends and great human beings. I remember band practice after school, and both Christmas parades in Yazoo City and in Greenwood.

I now look back upon those experiences with gratitude. However difficult they may have seemed at the time, we knew our teachers expected us to reach our full potential. If we failed to do so, our teachers would have felt they failed us. They were our drill instructors in a boot camp for a lifetime of learning. When my mind takes me back through the hallowed halls of old Yazoo City High, I see those teachers: Touchstone, Lester, DeCell, Watson, Beers, Vaughan, Williams, Hester, Parker, Clark, Jenkins, Caldwell, Massey, Rush, Kelly, and a dozen more, in front of their classes, excellence in teaching incarnate. I no longer fear them. I respect them, and want to belatedly thank them for having higher expectations of me than I had of myself. The message they pounded into my head finally got through: "William, if you apply yourself, there is no limit to what you can do and who you can become."

Yazoo, Yazoo, we are so proud of you. We hope we made you proud of us, as well.

CHAPTER 17

North Big 8 Champions

"Nobody in the game of football should be called a genius. A genius is somebody like Norman Einstein."
Joe Theismann, Former quarterback

If you are not from the South, you cannot fully appreciate how our passion for football is second only to religion in life's important priorities. Rev. Goodbody wasn't sure his parishioners didn't like football more than religion. Every minister in the state got at least one illustration from the Mississippi State-Ole Miss game. No one would dare schedule a meeting of any kind during that game. The state literally comes to a halt for three hours when that game is played. The winner relishes the win for a whole year, and the loser has to show humility to their acquaintances on the winning side.

It starts with Pee Wee football in elementary school. I can remember playing on the Blue team at Main Street Elementary in the fifth grade. My old buddy, Bobby David, played on the Red team from Annie Ellis. It was good to see him again, but tackling each other was a new experience.

The Green and White teams rounded out our four-team Pee Wee Conference. I can still remember the smell of those musty old jerseys, stored in the basement for a whole year. You could not convince me they were washed after last year's last game. Our helmets didn't match, and our football pants showed the effects of gridiron wars long forgotten. The junior high coaches would scout those games, looking for the new crop of talent coming along. The high school coaches scouted the junior high team, with an ever-vigilant eye toward next year.

High school football mattered in Yazoo City in the 1950s and 1960s. Stores closed on Friday afternoon for the parade down Main Street. The band marched, the majorettes twirled batons, the homecoming court rode in the back of convertibles, donated by the town's automobile dealers, waving to the adoring crowd. The cheerleaders chanted cheers of victory. The whole town worked itself into a frenzy, so that by 6:00 p.m., the bleachers at Crump Field were already near full in anticipation of the 7:00 p.m. kick-off. It still amazes me at how fast football season goes by; ten short weeks out of fifty-two. The remaining forty-two weeks are devoid of the magical air when it's pigskin time in Yazoo City.

During the 1950s, Yazoo City High dominated the Delta Valley Conference. We played teams like Rolling Fork, Drew, Rosedale, Ruleville and Indianola. But the Delta Valley was a second tier conference compared to the mighty Big 8. Sure, Drew produced a pretty good quarterback named Archie Manning, but even a blind hog roots up an acorn every once in a while. Oh, how we wanted to play the big teams: Greenwood, Meridian, Greenville, Tupelo, Columbus, Natchez, Biloxi, and the Jackson schools (Central, Provine and Murrah). We began scheduling one or two Big 8 schools each year, hoping to gain respectability. Then, in 1959, it happened. The Mississippi High School

Athletic Association divided the Big 8 into North and South Conferences. The winners of the North and South Big 8 would meet for the State Championship. The Association needed one more team for the North Big 8 to have an even number, and Yazoo City was selected. We felt like Green Bay, a small city, playing with the big guys. It was as if we had been selected to host the Olympics.

We needed a coach, a Vince Lombardi, who could make Yazoo City into a team respected from Clarksdale to Gulfport. The last thing we wanted was to be the doormat of the Big 8, the team everyone invited to be homecoming opponent. Yazoo City High School selected Eulas "Red" Jenkins, Southwest Junior College head coach, along with his assistant, Buzzy Clark. The pair had led Southwest to the State Junior College Championship the year before. As much as I would like to claim Coach Jenkins as a relative, his Jenkins ancestors and mine probably hadn't intersected since the days of "Old Jenkins Hill" in Washington, D.C. Red Jenkins knew, loved, lived, breathed and taught football. He was the consummate coach; just what Yazoo City was looking for.

Their first year in the Big 8, the 1959 Yazoo City Indians proved to be good ambassadors for the mighty Yazoo Indian nation. Averaging only 167 pounds per man, the Indians entered every game as underdogs. To everyone's surprise, Yazoo City won the first three games over Drew (21-0), Clarksdale (6-0) and a barnburner against Jackson Murrah (13-7). The first loss came at the hands of Greenwood 6-13, followed by a 7-7 tie to Vicksburg. Then the Indians caught their second wind, and ran off five straight wins over Columbus (27-7), Indianola (19-14), Cleveland (27-7) Columbia (32-0) and old Delta Valley archrival Canton (19-0). The last game of the season was a disappointing 7-21 loss to McComb, which cost the Indians the North Big 8 championship their very first year in the league. However, the Indians' impressive 8-2-1 record won the team and the town respectability in the world of Mississippi high school football.

The 1960 Yazoo City High School football season was one for the history books. The Indians entered the season with high hopes, following their surprisingly successful initial season. The Tribe picked up where they left off in 1959, winning their first four games against Belzoni (31-0), Clarksdale (27-7), a hard fought game against Jackson Murrah (12-0), and a win over Jackson Central (27-6).

The fifth game of the season against Greenwood came down to the final play. The score was 0-0. The first string quarterback, Jimmy Heidel, got hurt on the next to last play. Heidel had carried the team all the way down to the two-yard line with five seconds left on the game clock. Who was the backup? Jimmy Heidel was so good there was never a need to send in the backup. Even Coach Jenkins had to think for a minute. Then we could all see the "Oh no!" written on his face. T-Baby Calhoun was the backup. T-Baby had never taken a snap from center in a real game. For this last play of the game, Coach Jenkins explained in great detail what play he wanted T-Baby to call, a draw play where Rudy Porter would smash over left tackle. T-Baby wasn't good in following instructions, and called a different play, but the double reverse was so unexpected, it caught Greenwood Bulldogs off guard, and Rollo Moses raced into the end zone, just as the gun sounded, ending the game. The final score was Yazoo City 6, Greenwood 0. There was no need to kick the extra point. Yazoo City remained undefeated at the midpoint of the season.

Coach Jenkins didn't know whether to be angry at T-Baby, or kiss him. "T-Baby, why didn't you run the play I called?" "Well, Coach, I was so scared, I tried to remember all you said, but all I could do was remember seven and six. So I added them together and called out play 14." Coach

Jenkins paused, and then said, "But T-Baby, seven and six are 13, not 14." T-Baby looked at the ground, placed his right hand on Coach Jenkins' shoulder, spit some chewing tobacco out of his mouth, and said, "Coach, you know if I was as smart as you are, we might not have won that game."

Yazoo City's record remained perfect after beating Vicksburg 20-6. The first blemish of the season was a 0-0 tie against Greenville. That left the Indians 6-0-1, and atop the North Big 8 standings. The Tribe ran the table, winning the last three games of the regular season against Clinton (26-0), Columbia (20-0), and former archrival Canton (42-0). At the end of the regular season, Yazoo City's record was 9-0-1, good enough to win the North Big 8 Championship. Six of their ten games were shutouts, and no one scored more than seven points against the Indians.

The perfect ending to this story would be that Yazoo City High School went on to win the State championship. The Cinderella season came to an end in the championship game where Yazoo City High School met Jackson Provine, the South Big 8 Champions. The truth is Yazoo City lost the state championship game, 0-35. But forty years later, we still remember that magical season when Yazoo City High School got to play the big guys, and won the North Big 8 title, and won the respect of football fans all over Mississippi.

Then, in 1969, Yazoo City High School went 10-0, and won the State Championship with the help of All-American Larry Kramer. By then, I had graduated from Yazoo City High, and am not sure the Big 8 Conference was still in existence. Like many states, Mississippi developed a class system for high school athletics. It was a memorable decade of high school football in Old Yazoo.

CHAPTER 18

Child Labor

"Hard work never killed anybody, but why take a chance?"
Edgar Bergen "Charlie McCarthy" (1903-1978)

Hard work was one thing we learned early on our little Graball Hill farm. Everyone had to pull his or her end of the load. Failure to do hard work earned a person the title of lazy or worthless. Momma Roberts told us about a family she knew who were not only too lazy to plant and tend a garden, but too lazy to cook the food, and too lazy to "bring the fork to their mouth." She never did tell us what happened to them, but I suspect they starved to death.

My father enjoyed politics. He supported a particular candidate for governor, becoming his county campaign manager. Pop was generally respected in Yazoo County, and his efforts helped the candidate win not only the county, but the governorship. I accompanied my father on his rounds when we met an old acquaintance. Pop said, "I hope you support my candidate for governor." The friend replied, "I will, Pop, but you tell him when he is elected, I want one of them government 'sit down' jobs." Neither my father nor his friend ever heard back from the governor after his election. That's when I learned my first lesson in politics, and another lesson in work ethics.

I've often thought of that old man's request for a 'sit down' job. Daddy said he wasn't looking for work, just a paycheck.

So I learned sweat was a badge of honor. I must confess I never liked hard, manual labor. But I did my share. It was hard to say which was the worst job I ever had, but I learned something from each one of them—even if it was only that I never wanted to spend my life doing that.

Other than my chores on the farm and helping Daddy with his dry cleaning delivery route, my first paid position was working with my brothers at the Piggly Wiggly Grocery on Main Street. Norman got a job helping Mr. Haining in the meat market. Norman worked after school and all day Saturdays waiting on customers, learning to cut and wrap meat, sweep out the sawdust at the end of the day, and make home deliveries on the Piggly Wiggly bicycle. That bike was an icon around town. It had a big basket in front of the handlebars where jars of milk were placed for the milk route. Norman would load the bike down with milk and other items, making the bike weigh several times his weight. Balancing the bike while cycling it around town, especially up Broadway Hill, was backbreaking work. Norman stopped at the first house, popped down the kick stand, delivered one or two bottles of milk to the doorstep of the house, picked up the empty bottles, and returned to the bike for the remainder of the route. Completing the route took about two hours, and covered the whole town. The bike became lighter as the route progressed, which was good because he had spent most of his energy pedaling uphill with heavy milk bottles. As Norman completed the milk route, he would often encounter the drug store delivery boy making a sissy "one prescription delivery" somewhere around Grand Avenue and Fifteenth. The two would race back to Main Street, and even though Norman's energy was spent, he never lost that bike race. Norman got back to the store about 9:30 a.m., when most of the customers began arriving for their Saturday grocery shopping. If he left the store before midnight, he considered it a short day.

Norman's hard work earned the respect of Mr. Haining who gave Norman increasing responsibilities in the store. As Norman moved up, Mr. Haining asked Norman if he knew of anyone interested in taking over some of the chores, including the milk route. Without hesitation, Norman nominated our brother Tommy, who easily won the job. We counted on nepotism at the Yazoo City Piggly Wiggly. The milk route job was not competitively bid. The four Jenkins brothers owned that job for a decade. After Tommy was promoted, I got the job. Many days I thought I could not pedal another second and would collapse in the summer heat. I consider the day I passed the milk route on to my little brother Louis one of the happiest of my life.

I felt I was destined for something better than a laborer, and began the first of many life-long ventures as an entrepreneur. I took on a job as a Grit Newspaper delivery boy. Grit was a weekly tabloid newspaper published in Williamsport, Pennsylvania. It reported interesting news stories that reminded me of Paul Harvey's news. The paper had a national following, and I was not the only Grit delivery boy in Yazoo City. I would buy the papers weekly for about a nickel, and sell them to my customers for a dime. I figured if I could sell enough papers I could make a fortune. The papers arrived in a bundle on my doorstep Thursday afternoon, and I would walk all over Yazoo City, from Canal Street to Main to Broadway, College, and back to Canal. I learned a lot about business and economics selling Grit. Some of my regular customers were negligent in their payments, and I would have to eat the losses from my profits. I always ordered a few extra copies for new and impromptu sales, however, I could not return the unsold papers, so I had to be realistic in growing my business. Optimism and faith in my sales ability worked against me, and I soon returned to the ranks of wage labor.

Having hard working brothers was a boon to me. I picked up part time jobs at Mr. Coleman's Gas Station when Norman and Tommy worked there after the stint at Piggly Wiggly. They handled the management and auto repair work. I was the bookkeeper and helped pump gas when things got busy. We all worked at the Red Barn Mini Mart, an early version of a Seven-Eleven or Stop and Go.

One summer, I went to the employment office, and landed a job unloading Coca Cola trucks at the local bottling plant. In the 100-degree heat and high humidity of a Mississippi summer, that was without a doubt the worst job I ever had. After about four hours on the Coca Cola payroll, I quickly accepted another job offer at Southern Bag Corporation, where I worked three days flipping the ends of bags as they came off the conveyor belt, so they could be fed into the printing machine. It reminded me of the episode of "I Love Lucy" when Lucy was trying to keep up with the assembly line. I was about as successful as she was, and literally rubbed blisters down to the bone on the inside knuckle of my thumbs. My supervisor told me at the end of the eight-hour shift I had flipped over 10,000 bags. He was pleased. I wasn't. One may earn a living with one's back or one's brain, and I learned the wisdom of Ogden Nash's statement "*People who work sitting down get paid more than people who work standing up*." After my experience at Coca Cola and Southern Bag, I chose the "sit down" job.

When Owen Cooper offered me a work-study opportunity at Mississippi Chemical Corporation, I jumped at the opportunity. I was a gopher in the printing office, assigned to run various errands. One day, I received a call to gas up the company car and get ready to go to Dothan, Alabama to deliver and pick up papers, because MCC had purchased a plant there. I had never heard of Dothan. I ran into Jerry Clower in the MCC break room, who asked me where I was going. I said DOTH-an, Alabama. "Son," Mr. Clower said offering fatherly advice, "You better learn how to pronounce it right, or they will run you out of town. It's DOE-than, not DOTH-an." It was the first time I got to drive any measurable distance. I stayed in a motel in DOE-than for the first time in my life, and drove back to Yazoo City the next day. This was exciting and sure beat unloading Coca Cola trucks and flipping heavy bags! I even became the chauffeur for Mr. Cooper, driving him to speaking engagements and appointments all over Mississippi.

Hard work is the price we pay for our success. I learned that working smart enhances hard work. J. C. Penney said it well, "*Give me a stock clerk with a goal and I'll give you a man who will make history. Give me a man with no goals and I'll give you a stock clerk.*" The truth remains; there is no substitute for hard work if you want to move ahead in life.

CHAPTER 19

Yazoo City's First Shock Jock

"Live in such a way that you would not be ashamed to sell your parrot to the town gossip."
Will Rogers (1879-1935)

My first important job was at Yazoo City's first and foremost radio station, WAZF, 1230 on the AM dial. The studios were located "high atop the Taylor and Roberts Feed and Seed Building" on South Main Street. The folks from Rolling Fork who came to Yazoo City to do their Saturday shopping, referred to our two-story buildings as 'skyscrapers'. WAZF had 1940 vintage studios on the second floor of the Taylor and Roberts Building. The station was our source for music, news, sports, and entertainment.

Before I started school, I remember listening to the radio as my mother did her morning chores, hearing Arthur Godfrey play his ukulele. We heard the farm report, with the latest update on pig bellies. The weatherman reported, "Hot, humid," followed by more "hot, humid" and occasionally "rain". In the evening, we listened to "The Shadow", "Sergeant Yukon" and "The Green Hornet". I have yet to see a movie that frightened me more than those old radio episodes of "The Shadow". If the weather was clear, we could pick up WLAC out of Nashville, and listen to "The Grand Ol' Opry".

I was ten years old before I saw my first television. It was in the storefront window of the Yazoo Appliance Company on Main Street. Crowds would gather in the evening on the sidewalk to hear the news and see the new fangled gadget. Yazooans were slow to purchase televisions, because they cost a month's wages. We even ordered a cheap kit that promised to bring TV into our living room, but as the old saying goes, you get what you pay for.

When we lived on Graball Hill, we listened to WAZF over our RCA console tube radio. It was the nicest piece of furniture in our home. During the day, WAZF broadcast using 1,000 watts of power, which meant you could get a fairly strong signal anywhere in the county. At night, FCC regulations forced WAZF to lower its power to 250 watts, which meant the signal barely covered the city. If the wind was blowing just right at night, we could hear WAZF on Graball Hill.

The owner and program manager of WAZF, Mr. Highbaugh, had a penchant for such music as Guy Lombardo and his Royal Canadians, Mitch Miller and the Sing-along Gang, and Lawrence Welk's polka music. During the late 1950s, Yazoo City's youth were hungry for a different kind of music. My classmates could take only so much of Guy, Mitch, and Lawrence Welk's champagne bubbles. After much pleading and begging, WAZF relented, and permitted youth-oriented programs to be aired at 7:00 p.m., after the local news, and WAZF's most popular program, "Talk of the Town" with Lynette Mabry.

The first of these youth-oriented programs was "Darkness

on the Delta," and later a program called "Night Train". While you could only hear WAZF inside the city limits after sundown, I can assure you every person at Yazoo City High was listening every night. Night Train's format allowed youths to call in, request a song, and dedicate it to that special someone. The next day, the campus gossip was, "Did you hear that John dedicated 'Tear on My Pillow' to Mary last night?" WAZF only used first names, so we were left to guess who had a crush on whom, and did she know it, and was she interested? A few folks tried to play it cool, and pretend they didn't listen. But when someone said, "Linda dedicated 'Why Do Fools Fall in Love?' to Robert", they would chime in with, "No she didn't! It was Roy, not Robert! You must have wax in your ears!" The anonymity of common names made it all the more exciting, but when T-Baby called in and dedicated "Tossing and Turning" to Olivia, it just didn't work.

WAZF had a full staff: a general manager, salesman, news reporter, engineer, a part-time sports announcer and four disc jockeys. They operated much like a small television station today, covering everything from City Council meetings to the Rotary Club speaker.

When I was a junior in high school, Mrs. Parker, the English teacher, and Mr. Caldwell, my Speech teacher, encouraged me to persuade WAZF to host a weekly Yazoo City High School news program. They saw it as journalism; I saw it as my big opportunity. I would be the cub reporter, gathering news from around school, and read it in a live, fifteen-minute program on Thursday afternoon at 4:45 p.m.

I gathered news from the girl's softball game against Greenwood High, the results of the last debate tournament, and Yazoo City High's superior rating at the state band competition. It was easy, because I was in the band and on the debate team. (I decline to expose my source, nor the nature of my relationship, to the girl's softball team.)

WAZF thought the High School news program was a

good idea, and after all, 4:45 on Thursday afternoon was not exactly prime time, so what did they have to lose? My first Yazoo City High newscast went well, and Mr. Highbaugh asked me to stop by his office as I was leaving. "William, you have a good radio voice," he said. I blushed and thanked him. Public speaking has always come easy for me. I inherited this from my father, who could stand before his whole school and recite his notorious "Woodpecker" poem. Mr. Highbaugh asked me if I would be interested in recording some commercials for the station. A different voice would catch the listener's ear, he reasoned. Of course I was interested! But I was shocked to learn they would actually pay me. Heck, I would have paid them to be on the radio. When I told T-Baby, he said, "You have a face made for radio". Since T-Baby regularly whipped my sorry tail, I agreed with him.

One thing led to another, and one of the four disc jockeys eventually resigned. Mr. Highbaugh asked if I was interested in pulling a weekend shift and becoming the night DJ. That would leave me free to pursue my daytime education. I didn't have to think it over. All of a sudden, I was the Night Train jock, taking requests from my classmates, spinning the platters, and learning a good trade. And, I was following in the footsteps of another WAZF disc jockey that went on to greater fame, Willie Morris.

The weekend shift was a split shift. I signed on at 6:00 a.m. Saturday and worked to 10:00 a.m. The second announcer came in and worked the next four hours, and I returned for the 2:00 to 6:00 p.m. shift. Ditto for Sunday. The next weekend, we alternated, and I pulled the 10:00-2:00 and 6:00-10:00 shift. Needless to say, that didn't leave much time for a social life, not that girls were beating down my door.

The weeknight shift was a dream come true. I arrived at WAZF about 5:30 each afternoon to prepare for my 6:00 to 10:00 shift. 6:00 to 7:00 p.m. was the news block, followed by Night Train from 7:00 to 9:00, and then some weird soft music for the last hour. I guess Mr. Highbaugh thought all high school students should be in bed by 9:00, and the soft music would put them to sleep. But I had it on good authority that when Night Train ended, most of my classmates simply tuned in Dick Viondi at WWL in Chicago. We could get that 50,000-watt clear channel station in Old Yazoo. However, T-Baby and his more adventuresome friends headed to the honky tonk at Four Points to continue their entertainment.

The most difficult part of my night shift was patching Lynette Mabry through for her 6:30 "Talk of The Town" program. She phoned in her program from her home. Lynette was an institution in Yazoo City. Her program consisted of the social news, such as weddings, showers, and cotillion balls attended by the socialites and wannabee socialites of Yazoo City. The social ladder only had a few rungs in a town as small as ours.

Lynette had two mailboxes on her porch. One was for the regular U.S. mail; the other was for hand-delivered announcements of parties, guests visiting from out of town, and most commonly, weddings and wedding showers. The stories had what I thought were excruciatingly detailed accounts of the bridesmaid's dresses, the table centerpieces, and the corsages. But what did I know? It was the most listened to program in Yazoo City. Most people denied they listened to it, but it was the guilty pleasure of many Yazoo housewives as well as a surprising number of men.

Often, people would say, "I don't know how Lynette got all that information about my daughter's cotillion ball. Someone must have given it to her." The role of the second mailbox, Lynette once told me, was for people who would come up on her porch as late as midnight to drop off carefully typewritten stories. They always had their faces covered, and rushed away into the darkness. These were the same folks who listened carefully the next evening as Lynette read each word, whether grammatically correct or not, and then denied knowing how Lynette got the story, or why she thought "our little ol' story" was worthy of being read on "Talk of The Town". Deniability and false modesty are basic human traits needed to climb that social ladder.

Mrs. Mabry fascinated me. She was an older woman with a raspy voice that may have been due to years of chain smoking. She would frequently launch into a hacking cough during her program and I would try to hit the "cough" button so that the listeners would not have to hear that. Lynette Mabry was the first woman I knew who used "colorful language". I don't mean she used four letter words that you hear everywhere today, but for the 1960s, euphemisms were just as exciting as blurting out foul words. Often, when we chatted during the commercial break, Lynette would add personal comments about the people in the story she had just read; things she would never say on the air.

My job was to be sure Lynette's phone line was patched through, and when she said, "We'll be right back after this announcement from one of our sponsors," I was supposed to flip the switch to disconnect her microphone, which we called a "pot" and play a pre-recorded commercial. Usually Lynette would chat with me while the commercial aired.

One night, Lynette read about a wedding shower for a family who shall remain anonymous. I have long since forgotten the family's name, but I will never forget the night. During the commercial break, I must have been distracted and forgot to disconnect Lynette's line, the "pot", for the duration of the commercial.

"I can't believe she wore that tired old beige dress again to that shower," Lynette said, thinking she was speaking only to me. "Must be the only decent dress she owns. She's worn it a half dozen times." Neither of us knew her comments were going out all over Yazoo County. It was summer, and we were still at 1,000 watts at 6:30 p.m. "You think so, Mrs. Mabry?" I asked, just trying to hold up my end of the conversation. After all, what did I know about the protocol of such events? Those comments were followed with some of Lynette's observations about a few families, explaining to me the ebb and flow of the changing social order in our community.

I noticed a couple of the other phone lines were blinking. Dave Smith, my radio mentor, had given me explicit instructions not to answer other calls during Lynette's program, because if her line got disconnected, she would continue reading her news, and I could not call her back to let her know she was off the air. I later learned one of those calling was Mr. Highbaugh, the station manager, and the other one was my mother, both trying to tell me to "shut the pot," the radio expression to turn off the patched phone line. Alas, those desperate attempts to rescue me were fruitless.

The carnage did not end there. Every commercial break for the rest of the program was progressively more graphic, and Lynette used some of her colorful language to comment on the virtues and reputations of a few of the city's leading citizens. My ears were red, but I was mesmerized. I guess the whole darn town was, too.

At exactly 6:57 p.m., Mr. Highbaugh came rushing desperately up the stairs of the Taylor and Roberts Building screaming, "SHUT THE POT! SHUT THE POT!" Only then did I recognize my error, and stammered, "She…she only has three minutes left, let her finish."

If there had been Nielson ratings, that edition of "Talk of the Town," would have been "off the charts." That's another radio expression for an audience so high it could not be measured. Even the high school kids were calling their friends to tune in early, because there was something better than "Night Train" on WAZF.

Youth and inexperience played in my favor, in that both Mr. Highbaugh and Mrs. Mabry forgave my negligent oversight, mainly because "Talk of the Town" was the talk of the town.

Every merchant in town wanted to advertise on the program, making Mr. Highbaugh very pleased. Mrs. Mabry's reputation as a local legend was enhanced; Rev. Goodbody preached on the evils of gossip that Sunday; and I inadvertently became Yazoo City's first "shock jock" long before Howard Stern ever heard of the phrase.

CHAPTER 20

Darkness on the Delta

"Character is like a tree and reputation like its shadow.
The shadow is what we think of it;
the tree is the real thing."
Abraham Lincoln (1809-1865)

Darkness on the Delta
J. Levinson

When it's darkness on the delta
that's the time my heart is light,
When it's darkness on the delta
let me linger in the shelter of the night;
Fields of cotton all around me,
voices singin' soft and low,
Lord I'm lucky that you found me
Where the muddy Mississippi waters flow.

Lounging on the levee, Listenin' to the
nightingales way up above,
Laughter on the levee, no one's heart is
heavy,
All God's children got someone to love.

When it's darkness on the delta,
Only heaven is in sight,
When it's darkness on the delta,
let me linger in the shelter of the night.
Oh, Let me linger in the shelter of the night.

Our little house on Graball Hill sat at the base of the western slope, but high enough to provide us with some rather spectacular sunsets. As darkness set in over the Delta, I often listened to "Darkness on the Delta" on WAZF. The song became a hit in the 1940s. I attended a football game at my alma mater, Delta State University, a few years ago. At halftime the band played "Darkness on the Delta", the school song, and I felt the tears welling up in my eyes. To me, the Mississippi Delta is beautiful. I get strange looks from people when I say that. Some see it as flat, monotonous, swampy, and mosquito infested. I see it as enchanting, filled with all the mystery and allure of the bayou country.

Bound by the Yazoo River on the east and the Mississippi River on the west, the Mississippi Delta forms a crescent flatland between Memphis and Vicksburg. It is a land of contrasts, rich soil and pervasive poverty. Yet the Delta produced some of the finest artists and writers in America: B.B. King, Charley Pride, Muddy Waters, Hodding Carter, and Shelby Foote. James C. Cobb called the Mississippi Delta, "the most southern place on earth." The Delta still has the richest soil in the world, and is still producing some of the world's finest artists, writers, and entertainers.

The fine people of Yazoo City still practice the world's

oldest profession. Agriculture. I know what some people think is the world's oldest profession, but God commanded Adam to "till the ground," thus making agriculture, not that other profession, the world's oldest. God also commanded Adam and Eve to multiply, so I don't see how such rumors got started. Besides, is that any way to talk about your great-great-great...grandmother, Eve?

When my father was born at the beginning of the twentieth century, a majority of people worked on the farm. By the time the last century ended, less than ten percent of Americans worked on farms. Farming is a noble profession, and that makes the Delta a noble place.

My father was bi-vocational. In addition to running a dry cleaning establishment or selling cars, he ran our small farm until we moved to town in 1959. We learned early the discipline of farm life, rising before the sun, slopping the hogs, chopping wood, tending the stock, chopping weeds out of the gardens, killing hogs, raising chickens, baling hay, and canning food.

I remember we had a special garden for watermelons and cantaloupes. I asked my parents if I could have my own watermelon plot, and grow my very own big, red watermelon. They agreed, and that mound was the first land I ever called my own. I planted the seed, watered the mound, and went inside for the night. It was a full moon, and I remember not being able to sleep imagining eating my prize watermelon. It was going to be the biggest ever grown in Yazoo County, because I was going to nurture it and love it. No weed or bug was going to come within a mile of that mound. I got up and went back into the garden three times that night, with only the bright moon as my flashlight, to see if the seed had sprouted. Farm children must learn the difficult lesson of patience. Over the next few weeks, I would jump off the school bus as it dropped us off on Highway 49, and race straight to my watermelon mound. The plant took its time breaking the ground, and it looked sickly compared to the watermelons around it. Nevertheless, I brought water for it, fertilized it and gave it words of encouragement. Finally, the painful truth became obvious. My watermelon was not a watermelon at all. Instead of sitting down to devour a sweet juicy melon, I forced down my puny cucumber. The first lesson of the world's oldest profession is to be sure you plant the right seed to get the correct crop.

My farming instincts not totally dashed, I joined 4-H at school, and found we all had to complete a project to present at the Yazoo County Fair. Without consulting my parents, I agreed to raise 100 chicks. At age nine, I was a poultry farmer. Mother helped me build a brooder, a shed to raise the little chicks that arrived in cardboard boxes punched with holes. I fell in love with them all, and vowed I would never eat a one of them. We strung an electrical line from the house, and kept a light burning to keep the chicks warm on the colder nights. We had trays underneath their wire floor where we placed newspaper and collected their droppings. As Ross Perot once said, "Sooner or later, you have to clean out the barn."

I gave them each a name, although it was difficult to call the roll when they shuffled around. Some had distinguishing characteristics, such as "Down Feather" and "Red Beak". Identical twins or triplets would be a piece of cake compared to being the parent to 100 nearly identical chicks. The reality of life set in when some of the chicks died. That left 82 chickens. Then a fox got in the hen house, helped himself to two chicks, and killed another ten for good measure. That left 70 chickens. I posted Topey to guard the henhouse, but even Topey has to sleep. I went to the henhouse one morning and saw Topey fast asleep. Shugga had a feather hanging out her mouth, and a half dozen of her kittens were licking their paws. That made the count 58 chickens.

Rev. Goodbody was well known for his ability to put

away fried chicken when he visited various families in the church. Each Sunday, after services, he would go home with a family for lunch. Free Sunday lunch was a part of his compensation package. We obliged when it became our dubious honor to feed the parson. I backslid on my previous resolve, and six chickens were fried for Sunday dinner. "Now wait until the Reverend has had his fill before you take any of the good pieces," Mother warned us. I thought the preacher was going to eat every piece of chicken Mother cooked. I only got one wing and a neck. That left 52 chickens.

I inadvertently became Yazoo City's first free-range chicken farmer. Free-range chickens are let loose, and may roam, rather than exist cooped up in a brooder or chicken house all their lives. It's quite popular and politically correct these days, especially in California. The only problem is, once they got out, I wasn't able to get them all back in. The escaped chickens formed a colony and their great-great-great grandchicks still roam Graball Hill, much like the Kauai wild roosters in Hawaii. I lost count at this point, but only a dozen or so chickens returned to the coop.

One day I met T-Baby on the dusty road that led up Graball Hill. I was carrying a sack. "What ya' got in the sack?" he asked me. "Chickens" I replied. "Will you give me one of them if I guess how many?" he asked. Since I was scared to make him angry, I replied, "Heck, I'll give you both of them." T-Baby said, "Cool, I'll guess you have five chickens." I said, "Dang, you're good. Here are two of them, and I'll be back in a minute with the other three." That left seven chickens.

By the time the County Fair rolled around, I had three chickens left. I entered Bent Feather, Pully Bone and Broken Beak in the 4-H contests. Not surprisingly, I did not win a blue ribbon or even an honorable mention. However, as 4-H had anticipated, I learned many lessons on Delta farming and Delta life.

CHAPTER 21

Hello Darlin'

"I don't know anything about music.
In my line you don't have to."
Elvis Presley (1935-1977)

Conway Twitty, whose real name was Harold Lloyd Jenkins, was my third cousin. We both descended from Aaron Jenkins, born in 1799, and who moved to Mississippi about 1830. Conway was born at Friar's Point, near Clarksdale, and began singing rock and roll songs in the 1950s, about the same time Elvis Presley, another Mississippian, began his meteoric career. Conway later switched to country music, but one of his biggest hits was "Hello Darlin'" which he performed many times on American Bandstand.

I went to Twitty City, in Hendersonville, Tennessee, where Conway built homes for his mother, brother, and children. Twitty City also had a theater where he performed two shows a night when he was not on the road making other performances. I asked Conway to tell me about his powerful effect on women and the secrets of love. He said, "Come, and I will show you." Backstage between performances, Conway asked if I saw a certain woman who walked down to the edge of the stage, and began throwing undergarments at him. Of course I did, no one could have missed her. "She shows up at almost every show, and I have a room full of that lady's underwear. I think she keeps Victoria's Secrets in business." I saw his powerful effect over women, but as much as I have tried, I cannot replicate it.

Conway told me he hated this story, but it's a good one, so I'm telling it anyway. A handsome young preacher moved to town, who looked remarkably like Conway Twitty. He knocked on the door of one of his parishioners, an older lady, who came to the door and said, "Oh my, it's Conway Twitty!" "No ma'am," the young preacher said, "Folks tell me I look like him, but I'm the new parson." The scene repeated itself several times until the preacher knocked on one door, and a very beautiful and remarkably healthy looking young woman answered the door wearing only a towel, obviously just out of the shower. "Conway Twitty!" the woman exclaimed, throwing open her arms, and losing her towel. The young parson thought, why fight it? "Hello Darlin'".

As I have grown older, having long since passed beyond the days of puppy love, I have come to realize the importance of having a darlin' to say hello to first thing every morning and last thing every night. My siblings were my mentors and role models. I was still a bit young to know all the details about Ellen meeting Rayford Kinard. They loved each other very much, and gave me my first nephews, Donnie and David. I also don't have all the details on Norman meeting Frankie Hilderbrand from Satartia in Yazoo County, so they will sigh in relief that I will not embarrass them. I thank them for giving me Doug as a wonderful nephew, and Kim as an outstanding niece.

My remaining siblings will not escape me "telling on"

them. My education in matters of love included an assignment as chaperone for my sister, Marietta, and her boyfriend, Ron Wilkinson. Marietta and Ron were in the same class and began dating in high school. After high school, Marietta went to Gilfoy School of Nursing in Jackson, and Ron went to a community college in the Delta. The relationship seemed to be getting pretty serious, and Mother wasn't entirely pleased, because she wanted Marietta to finish nursing school and not be thinking about settling down yet.

On Sunday afternoons, Ron wanted to drive Marietta to Jackson so they could spend as much time as possible together since they would not see each other until the next weekend. Mother couldn't spend time physically sitting between the two, but decided on the next best thing. She allowed Ron to drive Marietta to Jackson, but only if I went along as chaperone. Mother figured that would put a damper on their budding relationship. Those were much more conservative times. I was okay with this arrangement because I thought it provided me an opportunity to get back at Marietta for all the chores she assigned me when Mother was not at home.

I have to give Ron credit though, for being resourceful. He said, "William, I have two dollars here, and if you want to take a nap on the back seat of the car, feel free to do so." Heck, I'm no fool. I said, "Ok, but you have to teach me all you know about women and love." I took the two dollars, and went fast asleep. I wasn't too worried about defending my sister's honor, either. She could whip my tail and Tommy's tail at the same time. If Ron tried to pull something she didn't want, I suspect she could take care of herself. But from where I was taking my Sunday afternoon naps, it didn't seem to me that either one of them had fighting on their minds. Like Tommy, Ron could drive and kiss at the same time. I was impressed. Every so often, I sneaked a peek, and filed Ron's technique away for future reference. I wanted to be prepared just in case the opportunity ever presented itself for me to kiss one of my girlfriends while driving. Ron and Marietta liked Johnny Mathis music, but at least once I heard Ron whisper, "Hello Darlin'".

Mother will be disappointed in me that I wasn't the kind of chaperone she expected. But two dollars wasn't bad for taking a nap, and I volunteered for chaperone duty until they got married. After nearly four decades, they are still married, and I got two outstanding nephews, Jeff and Joey, out of the deal. So, all's well that ends well. I watched as my future brother in law worked his charm, but I still couldn't get it to work for me.

Tommy had a Corvette Sting Ray and wasn't afraid to use it. So I asked Tommy to tell me the secrets of love and women. He said, "Watch me, and take notes." Before Tommy began dating Tiffie Moses, the girl he would marry, rumors had it he was on dates in Belzoni. Tommy was very handsome, charming, and with a Sting Ray, I bet the Delta girls took notice. He was a gentleman and never talked about those dates, but one evening, I was sitting in my car alone at a hamburger drive-in at Cleveland, Mississippi. There were two girls in a car directly across from me who were giggling. One of them finally got out of the car, walked over to my car, leaned over…and I do mean, leaned over…and said, "You look like Tommy Jenkins from Yazoo City. Are you his brother?" I felt the same way I did that day I caught Nancy at recess at Main Street Elementary and asked her for a kiss. "Uh oh, what do I do now?" "As a matter of fact, I am," I said nervously. "My girlfriend and I were wondering, would you like a date tonight?" So I said the only thing I could think of, "Hello Darlin'." I'll end the story right there for the benefit of the children in the audience. All I will say is it was great to have an older brother like Tommy. He never talked about his dates in Belzoni and other places around the Delta, so I never learned exactly what Tommy did, but apparently he did it very well. But finally, I was beginning to get some clues.

Then, there was Louis. Louis was a card-carrying member of Spanky's He-man Woman Hater's Club. He said many times, "Women are nothing but an accident looking for a place to happen." Maybe he was disgusted with us making "goo-goo" eyes at our "steadies". Plus, in addition to being industrious, Louis was all business, and extremely frugal. He knew that you could either have money or a girlfriend, and he chose money. Oh, don't get me wrong, Louis was very popular; he was just so darn mature for his age. Another one of Louis' lines was, "I'm going to be a rich old bachelor, and raise my children to be the same." We believed him.

Then it happened. Louis went off to Holmes Junior College, following, I wish to point out, in the footsteps of his older brother. One night, Louis called home and spoke to Mother. "I met her," Louis said. "Met who?" Mother asked. "I met the girl I am going to marry. I saw her walking across campus today." "Who is she?" Mother asked, startled, but trying to maintain composure. "I don't know, but I am going to marry her," Louis said. And he did. That's a "Hello Darlin'" even Conway would be proud of. Louis and Kathy are the parents of my two wonderful nieces, Kendy and Krystal. And did I mention Louis is good at business? I would say when the love bug finally bit; Louis was a man of action. Another lesson I learned that served me well many years later.

My life has taken some twists and turns along the way, and I confess to being guilty of looking for love in all the wrong places, but I finally found the love of my life in Anita. We were married three weeks to the day after we met, and over a decade later our love is stronger than when we wed. Without Anita, I wouldn't have my daughter, Deanna, nor would I be Paw Paw to Tak and Kat, and I wouldn't have Chris as my son. And without Anita, I wouldn't have my best friend.

For whatever it is worth, I would like to share my knowledge with any young men who are looking for advice on matters of the heart as I did. Here are my top ten tips for happiness in my relationship.

1. Anita is the boss.
2. Anita is always right.
3. Don't make Anita angry.
4. Anita has a long memory.
5. Anita doesn't like surprises.
6. Tell Anita you love her, often.
7. Show Anita you love her, often.
8. Anita doesn't like it when I leave the seat up.
9. Electronically deposit your paycheck into Anita's account
10. If you ever doubt any of these, start again with No. 1.

This may sound a little harsh, but I am healthier, happier, richer, and more productive than I ever imagined I could be. I can tell you this for certain; these rules have brought me over a decade of marital bliss. And did I mention, my mother *loves* Anita?

Anita sometimes asks me to sing to her. I am not a good singer, but I'll do whatever she asks.

"Hello Darlin'"

CHAPTER 22

Nostalgia Ain't What It Used To Be

"People seem not to see that their opinion of the world is also a confession of their character."
Ralph Waldo Emerson (1803-1882)

Will Rogers said it well; "Things ain't what they used to be and probably never was." One may afford the luxury of nostalgia only when it is absolutely certain there is no possibility of returning to the good old days.

My mental journey back to Yazoo City is by no way a call to return to the "Good Old Days," because that would be impossible. All I have to do to disavow myself of such a notion is to go camping. I must admit the memories of the days on Graball Hill conveniently forget the hardships we endured to get through those experiences. This is where a bad memory comes in mighty handy.

Among my favorite childhood memories were nighttime at our old house on Graball Hill, after supper. We called it supper, not dinner. Dinner was our noon meal. Pop was a disciple of Benjamin Franklin, who said, "Early to bed and early to rise, makes a man healthy, wealthy and wise." Pop worked from sun to sun, 6:00 a.m. to 6:00 p.m. As we played in the front yard, we watched for his car turning off Highway 49 and up the long dusty driveway. "Daddy's home, Daddy's coming," we would shout, as if Mother needed any notice to start setting the table. He was as predictable as a clock. Having our tummies filled with Mother's good cooking, Pop would head off to bed. This was Topey's favorite time as well, because he got the scraps from the table. Like me, he thought Mother was the best cook in Yazoo County.

While Mother and the girls washed and put away the dishes, we started a familiar chant: "Tell us some stories, Daddy, tell us some stories." That was our way of getting permission to crawl up in his bed, and listen to the stories of his childhood in Calhoun County. Today, I find it difficult to comprehend, but I distinctly remember thinking how primitive turn of the century Mississippi was for my father. Never mind that we were living in a primitive environment of our own, we at least knew there were modern conveniences.

Pop was a master storyteller. He transported us in both miles and time back to his boyhood. He had a great sense of humor, and always worked in a good laugh. We never tired of his stories. We heard the same ones over and over. "Tell us that panther story," we requested, and for the next ten minutes or so, he captivated us as we heard the story about Old Jim's mule-drawn wagon coming home without Jim. Pop and his brothers retraced the wagon's route, and found Old Jim's body on the side of the road, mauled by a panther that waited for him to pass underneath a limb that crossed the road. There were "boo" lines, where Pop would elicit goose bumps on top of our goose bumps as we awaited the "gottcha" line, usually delivered in a shout. We knew it was coming, both what and when, but he never ceased to scare the dickens out of us. That's the mark of a great yarn spinner. Occasionally, we would remind him that he left out a certain part. We could tell the story ourselves, but there was something magical about Pop telling it.

"Tell another one," we implored as soon as he finished. "It's time for bed." "No, no, Pop. One more, just one more." "OK, but this is the last one." And then he took off for another fifteen-minute journey back in time and space, telling the story of how he and his brothers scared the socks off a nervous friend, Abe. They ran a pipe down the bank of a trail and hid it with leaves. After dark, when Abe was walking nervously home, they spoke through the pipe, which served as a megaphone, "Abe. (Pause) You've been a mighty, mighty, mean boy." "Who's there," Abe asked, looking in all directions at once. "Abe. (Pause) You've been a mighty, mighty, mean boy." "I know you are there. Who are you?" About that time, Pop and his brothers began rustling in the leaves and making awful noises. They laughed as Abe ran out of both his shoes and socks on his way home. By now, Louis and I were having trouble keeping our eyes open. I was usually good for two and a half stories, and awoke in my own bed, not sure how I got there, but was assured my transport was an act of love.

As I enter my senior years, I have come to recognize that my nostalgia for the days on Graball Hill is rooted in my father's nostalgia for his childhood in Calhoun County. I learned at the foot of his bed a love and respect for place and time, for family and friends, for memories and emotions. As I accompanied Pop on many trips back to Calhoun County, I expected to see the panther that killed Old Jim, or to see Abe's shoes on the side of the road. I lived vicariously through his memories, knew people I had never met, and was familiar with places I had never seen.

As I walk with my four-year-old granddaughter, Kat, around Nana Anita's rock and flower garden, I wonder if I am planting the seeds of experiences she will one day grow into her memories as her good old days. I will never know which pebble she will save, which petal she will treasure, anymore than my father knew which of his stories I would remember over a half century later.

Nostalgia ain't what it used to be. What I remember most was the warmth, the tenderness, and the love.

CHAPTER 23

Take Me Back To Ol' Yazoo

"A man travels the world over in search of what he needs and returns home to find it."
George Moore

Andy Razaf, the "Prince of Madagascar", wrote the words to the song, "Old Yazoo". He was the author of hundreds of songs, including "Honeysuckle Rose" and "Ain't Misbehavin'". Jazz greats like Fats Waller, who wrote the music to "Old Yazoo," Louis Armstrong, Ella Fitzgerald, and Ethel Waters performed Andy Razaf songs throughout their careers.

Take me back to Ol' Yazoo.
Everything up here is new.
I can't stand it, just must land it.
Going back to Ol' Yazoo.

Everything you do,
People got their eyes on you.
It's compelling, hear me yelling.
Going back to Ol' Yazoo.

How long will I have to wait,
Just standing at the station gate?
I'm broken hearted, got to get started
Going back to Ol' Yazoo.

Broken hearted, got to get started.
Going back to Ol' Yazoo.

In the early 1930s, the Boswell Sisters recorded Razaf's, "Old Yazoo". It started out, "Take me back to Old Yazoo." Thomas Wolfe's axiom says, "You can't go home again". When I return to Yazoo City to see my mother, sisters and brothers, and extended family, I test what Wolfe said. In one way he was correct, because the Yazoo City I knew as a child is not the one I find. The town has changed, and so have I. But the places are still familiar, the people are wonderful, and the memories are unchangeable. Those of us who have the privilege of place; that geographic point of reference we call home, can test how far we have traveled, much as a sailor returns to the shore to see how far out to sea he has been. I've enjoyed quite a life journey. But there is nothing like going home.

When I go back to Old Yazoo, I always hope to see the beautiful Orioles eating at my sister's bird feeder. I hope to eat some catfish, cooked only as Mississippians know how. I hope to hear rain on my mother's roof. I want to see Main Street again. I want to drive by Annie Ellis and Main Street Elementary, the Junior and High Schools I attended. I want to see the old church again. Mostly, I want to rest and laugh and love and to be loved, and get nostalgic for the good old days I took for granted while growing up in Old Yazoo. And when it is all done, I test Wolfe's axiom one more time. Will I be able to "go home again"...my home in San Diego?

But even if I could go back to the Yazoo City of the 1950s and 1960s, it would not be the same. As time made its relentless march, some of those closest to my heart and mind have moved permanently away.

Tommy died in an automobile accident in November 1971. How ironic that Tommy, who won so many trophies drag racing his Corvette Sting Ray, should die so young in an automobile wreck. I cannot think of anyone I would have trusted more at the wheel than Tommy. He was only 24 years old, and left Tiffie a widow, and his 18-month old son, Todd, and three month old daughter, Paige, without their father. Todd is the mirror image of his father. One of the joys of my older age is talking with Todd and Paige about their father. I don't think Tommy had an enemy in the world. His love was magnetic. He loved going with Mr. Haining to Cherokee, North Carolina, and mining for precious stones, such as sapphires and rubies. He found a special one, and gave it to Mother, who had it made into a ring, which she now treasures. At his funeral, Tommy's boss used a gemologist metaphor when he said, "Tommy was a diamond in the rough."

While Tommy's death was sudden and shocking, Ellen's death was slow and painful. She died of a brain tumor in 1987. If I have my choice, I would prefer to go as Tommy did. Ellen's illness and death were equally ironic. She was a nurse, and a pillar of the community in Lauderdale County where she and Rayford lived, farmed, and raised their sons, Donnie and David. Diseases of the mind, such as brain tumors, dementia, and Alzheimer's disease, are the cruelest of all, because whereas other diseases take one's life, these take one's memories, and one's personality. One of the saddest days of my life was when I went to see Ellen, shortly before she died, and realized she did not know who I was. All her memories of Graball Hill and our loving family were gone.

Ellen's laughter and sense of humor were infectious. I remember one Christmas when we were grown that Ellen made an announcement: "As the oldest Jenkins child, I want to give a present to the youngest." I will never forget the look on Louis' face when he opened the gift, and slowly held up the largest pair of ladies' bloomers I have ever seen. "Thanks, Ellen, I guess I needed these," Louis said about the gag gift as our whole family roared in laughter. Not to be outdone, Louis surprised Ellen by wrapping those bloomers in a beautiful box and giving them back to Ellen the next year. The exchange went on for several Christmases to follow, and became a family tradition we all anticipated. Ellen was the person who organized the ladies of the church to take food to families in grief and in need. She directed and catered more weddings than anyone can count. After Ellen's death, her church named the fellowship hall the Ellen Ann Jenkins Kinard Hall. Did I tell you Ellen was an angel? I expect Ellen is on some heavenly committee, organizing a social. When we all get back together, I expect she will have a present for Louis, oldest to youngest, and we will all laugh as the Christmas tradition carries on.

Pop lived to a good old age of 87, and died on Valentine's Day 1989. He became totally blind and spent his last decade in a dim world, surrounded by those who loved him. He had to memorize the layout of the house, and feel his way as he walked from the bedroom to his favorite chair and back again. I am certain in the perfect vision of his mind; he revisited the days of his childhood in Calhoun County, attended Gospel and Sacred Harp singings, and relived our family days on Graball Hill. His memories remained sharp all his life, and when I asked questions about family genealogy, he almost never failed to come up with the right name or place I needed to fill in the missing branches of our family tree. I do not remember if it was before or after Pop's blindness I began doing what many sons and fathers find difficult. I told Pop "I love you," and gave him a hug and a kiss on his brow every time we visited, which was often. He always responded, "I love you, too, William." Like the apostle Paul, Pop can now say, "I saw through a glass dimly, but now I can see face to face." Fathers speak blessings or curses upon their children. Pop spoke blessings upon us with his word of love, "I have a million dollar family." He's finally a millionaire, walking the streets of gold, and living in his well earned heavenly mansion.

Long gone also, are my cousin Conway, Momma and Daddy Roberts, Aunt Minnie and Uncle Wilburn, and of course, Topey. Also many of my friends, teachers, neighbors and others that shaped my life and contributed to my treasured memories. Every letter and phone call from home usually brings news of the latest passing of someone I knew. And I increasingly dread the call that will herald the passing of one of my immediate family. While there is the occasional good news of births of the future generation of "Jenkins" from my many nieces and nephews, these are new relatives I will never have the privilege of knowing in the same rich and rewarding way I knew my past relatives.

Sometimes I fantasize about retiring in Yazoo City, but in my heart of hearts I know it would be a disappointment to me because I would always be trying to make it be what it was forty years ago. I would not be able to appreciate it for what it is today. I do hope there are little boys and girls (perhaps the children of my nieces and nephews?) who are today romping the streets of a Yazoo City, or any wholesome town, and experiencing the same types of adventures, education, and mistakes I had. And especially, making the same memories.

I don't get back to Old Yazoo as much as I would like. But through the blessings of my mind, I can visit the cotton fields and Graball Hill whenever I wish.

CHAPTER 24

Thank God Those Cotton Pickin' Days Are Over

"Thank God for poverty. That makes and keeps us free and lets us go our unobtrusive way, glad of the sun and rain; upright, serene, humane; contented with the fortune of a day."
William Bliss Carman

As a young man, I lived for three years in Green Bay, Wisconsin. Maybe there was a hidden desire to go somewhere the kudzu could not grow. The winters in Green Bay were as cold as the summers in Mississippi were hot. At least the change was interesting…for the first two years. By the third year, I experienced what some call cabin fever. After all, you don't see the ground for six months.

I recall one of the stories a Wisconsin dairy farmer, Ollie Swenson, told me. He once had to get up at three in the morning to milk his cows, even when it was forty degrees below zero. Then one of his brothers told him about a new fangled gadget called a milking machine. You just attach it to the cows', well you know, those things, and it milks the cow for you. He wanted to give it a try, so he hooked the milking machine up to his prize cow, Nellie, and went about doing other chores. At first he thought it was a great labor saving device. Look at all the work he could do by not having to milk the cows the conventional way. Unfortunately, Ollie got carried away doing his chores and forgot Nellie and the milking machine until late afternoon. He rushed back to the barn to find Nellie passed out on the floor. He quickly called the vet who asked how Nellie looked. "To be honest," Ollie said, "she looks pooped, but proud." Like Nellie, I may be pooped, but I am proud to have lived on Graball Hill and in Yazoo City, sharing some of the best experiences life has to offer with some of the most genuine, loving people God ever created.

My mother's parents, Momma and Daddy Roberts, lived in Yazoo City for a while. We continued to exchange visits after they settled in Kingsport, Tennessee. Those thirteen-hour trips to Kingsport are among my most vivid childhood memories. Can you imagine seven children asking; "Are we there yet?" for thirteen hours? Those were the days before Interstate highways.

Both Momma and Daddy Roberts had wonderful senses of humor. "Ida," Daddy Roberts once said, "when you get to be eighty years old, I'm going to trade you in on four twenties!" "You wouldn't know what to do with them," she replied. Daddy Roberts refused to set his watch back to central time when he visited from Kingsport. At five o'clock, he would look at his watch and say, "Well, it's six o'clock at home." That fascinated and confused us. How could time be one hour ahead of Yazoo City? Momma Roberts could say the ABC's backwards, beginning ZYX. I often tried but never made it past X.

One day, Daddy Roberts said, "I think women are just getting too soft these days, what with washing machines and gas stoves. I can remember the days when a nine months pregnant woman would get up before daylight, cook breakfast, milk the cows, go out to the fields and pick cotton until noon. Then she would go back to the house, give birth, and be back in the cotton fields before the sun went down. Yep, those were real women." Momma Roberts looked at him and said, "Yes, and thank God those cotton pickin' days are over."

In some ways, I, too, am glad those cotton pickin' days are over. I don't miss outdoor toilets, hot summers without air conditioning, or running water from the cistern to the house in a bucket. I love technology and the internet and improved medical care. I am spoiled by my 300-channel TV, two-minute coffee maker, and spa bath tub. But, in other ways, it is too bad those days are gone. Too bad there aren't many big families anymore. Too bad folks don't have the values or priorities they had back then.

I miss Main Street on Saturday nights. I miss Little Mingo, Topey and T-Baby, playing with my brothers and sisters and Bobby David. I miss the smell of magnolias and bacon cooking on a wood stove. I miss Friday night football and listening to Mrs. Mabry on "Talk of the Town". I miss Rev. Goodbody's sermons and Aunt Minnie's laughter. I miss hanging out with my friends before the first bell at Yazoo City High, and dragging Main Street on Friday night. I miss listening to Daddy telling us stories as we fell asleep in his bed while Mother put away the dishes.

And yes, sometimes I even miss the kudzu, because what would Yazoo City have been without it?

Epilogue

(Reprinted with permission of the Associated Press)

Army posts fight botanical beast kudzu
Rapid-growing vine attacking bases
By Bill Baskervill

Associated Press
Aug. 23, 2002

FORT PICKETT, Va. - In little more than 100 years in the United States, kudzu has marched across farm fields, shoved aside native plants and disrupted ecosystems with its smothering blanket of green leaves.

Now, the nearly indestructible vine is taking on the Army.

It has already overrun training areas at Fort Pickett, and Pentagon officials say it is an ongoing problem at Fort Bragg, N.C., the Redstone Arsenal and Anniston Army Depot in Alabama and Fort Jackson, S.C.

How bad is it? Infantrymen, Humvees, armored personnel carriers and even the 68-ton M-1 Abrams tank, which laid waste to Iraqi armor during the Gulf War, steer clear of kudzu fields.

"When you get out there, it can tangle you up, wrap around you," said Paul Carter, the Fort Pickett forester and resident expert on the tenacious plant. "You can't see where you're stepping."

Then there's the problem of what lies beneath it: The thick cover is a cool canopy for the poisonous copperhead snake, and no tank driver in his right mind would venture into it because it renders the terrain invisible.

"This is a road," said Carter, pointing to the ground as he waded into a 20-acre field of 5-foot-high kudzu. Nothing can be seen except a sea of kudzu stretching to a line of distant trees, which are also being overrun.

"It's got the entire field," he said. "It just kind of engulfs everything."

Kudzu is native to China, made its way into Japan and was introduced in the United States in the late 1800s, originally as a climbing ornamental plant at upscale homes.

Then, in the 1930s, the Agriculture Department decided kudzu could be used for erosion control and distributed 85 million kudzu seedlings in the South.

It was later discovered that kudzu's erosion control properties were limited because its vines grow horizontally and slightly above ground, and that they branch out as much as 2 feet a day.

The USDA removed kudzu from its list of recommended cover crops in 1953 and in 1970 declared it a weed. Since then, efforts have been aimed at eradication.

Carter has burned it, sprayed it with herbicides and even pulled up individual plants by hand.

A concerted herbicide assault forced one field of kudzu into retreat after it enveloped an abandoned, obsolete tank.

Now, a year later, it is reoccupying the field. Across Fort Pickett, it occupies 128 acres at 18 sites.

The service doesn't keep track of the cost of controlling the growth, but Fort Pickett soon will have a $58,000 contract for kudzu control. Redstone Arsenal treats 300 acres of kudzu at up to $400 an acre.

Nationwide, the government estimates the loss in agriculture production is about $7.4 billion annually because of invasive plants that cover about 100 million acres. Kudzu has spread to New England, Illinois and the Pacific Northwest.

At Fort Hunter Liggett, an Army Reserve training center in California, the problem is the thorny yellowstar thistle, which "is so thick and grows so aggressively it actually hinders the mission considerably," said Bill Woodson, an Army natural resources specialist at the Pentagon.

"Soldiers just can't go in there," he said, and paratroopers "don't like to land in the thistle."

A task force was created under a 1999 executive order to find ways to stop the attack by invasive, non-native plants such as kudzu, yellowstar thistle, spotted knapweed, Chinese privet, purple loosestrife and the tree of heaven.

Jim Miller, a kudzu expert with the Forest Service, said the vine has to be treated persistently with herbicides for four to 10 years to gain control or kill it.

Kudzu usually reappears, mainly because of a robust root system that burrows up to 14 feet into the ground. Experts say future success in battling it may lie with biological control in which native insects and fungi that feed on the plant.

Forest Service scientists are already in China surveying kudzu's natural enemies.

For now, Miller said the target should the plant's root crown, "the heart and brains of kudzu" that lies just underground.

"If you can kill that, the size of the root doesn't matter," he said.

APPENDIX

Yazoo Glossary

Annie Ellis Elementary School
Located on Grand Avenue, Yazoo City built this school about 1950 to accommodate the baby boom after World War II, when Main Street Elementary was no longer adequate to house the growing population.

Armory, National Guard
The National Guard Armory was the site of many dances and social events for the town's youth.

Barbour, Haley (1947-)
Yazoo City native son elected Governor of Mississippi in 2003. Barbour served as an advisor to President Ronald Reagan for two years as Director of the White House Office of Political Affairs. From 1993 to January 1997, he served two terms as chairman of the Republican National Committee.

Bella Vista
Name first given to a modern subdivision of homes begun in

1958, located between the western slope of Graball Hill and Highway 49. This was the site of the author's childhood.

Benton
One of the earliest communities in the region, Benton was once the county seat of Yazoo County. Benton is located east of Yazoo City on Highway 16.

Bentonia
Community on Highway 49 south of Yazoo City.

Big 8
Name of the high school athletic conference for the largest high schools in Mississippi.

Blackjack
Community in southeast Yazoo County.

Broadway Street
This is a key street for traffic traveling west of Yazoo City on Highway 49W. Broadway is the last hill for traffic headed west into the Delta. Confederates built a shipyard at the top of Broadway during the Civil War and rolled ships down the hill on logs to the banks of the Yazoo River for deployment. The Yankees burned the shipyard. Broadway Street is the site of many Victorian style homes.

Cairo, USS
Name of Union ship sunk in the Yazoo River north of Vicksburg in 1862 by Confederate mines. The ship was recovered a century later.

Cannonball Express
Name of the locomotive in which Casey Jones died in 1900 near Vaughan in Yazoo County. (See Jones, Casey).

Chickasaw
Major Native American tribe that occupied portions of North Mississippi.

Chieftan, The
Name of the Yazoo City High School athletic team bus during the 1950s and 1960s. The bus was retired in 1966.

Chito, Mingo
Name given for the senior chief of the Yazoo Native Americans. The name literally means "Big Chief". Also the name given to the Yazoo City High School yearbook.

Choctaw
Name of the most significant tribe of Native Americans in Mississippi.

Clower, Jerry (1926-1998)
Born at Liberty, Mississippi in South Mississippi, Jerry Clower moved to Yazoo City to work for Mississippi Chemical Company as a fertilizer salesman. He became famous as a country music entertainer, telling humorous stories of his childhood. For most of his adult life, Jerry Clower called Yazoo City home, and made the community famous through his stories. Jerry Clower was a dedicated Christian layman, and took pride in the fact he could tell funny stories without using vulgar language.

Cooper, Owen (1908-1986)
Industrialist and philanthropist. Founder of Mississippi Chemical Corporation. Owen Cooper also served as president of the Southern Baptist Convention, one of a very few laymen to serve in that capacity for the nation's largest Protestant denomination.

Country Club
Site of golf course, club house, and swimming pool where many social events are held. Located on Highway 49 just north of the Bella Vista subdivision and Graball Hill.

Crump Field
Name of the Yazoo City High School football field on Calhoun Avenue.

Doak's Stand, Treaty of
Treaty signed in 1820 that opened the Indian lands of North Mississippi and the Delta to white settlers.

"Darkness on the Delta"
Name of song written by J. Levinson. School song adopted by Delta State University.

Delta, The Mississippi
A crescent region between Memphis and Vicksburg bordered on the west by the Mississippi River and on the east by the Yazoo River. The area is a flat swampy area of fertile soil created by annual flooding of the Mississippi River before the levee system was put in place. The Delta is known for it's rhythm and blues culture.

Eden
Community located in northern Yazoo County.

Fire of 1904
Legendary fire that destroyed most of Yazoo City. (See also Witch, The Yazoo)

Flashlight, The
Name of the Yazoo City High School newspaper at the time Willie Morris was the high school editor. The school paper

received national awards for excellence.

Four Points
Intersection of US Highways 49E, 49W and 16. Popular hang out for high school students in the 1950s and 1960s.

Goose Egg Park
Popular name given to Ricks Park, and oval park on Grand Avenue.

Graball Hill
Hill located at the northern edge of Yazoo City overlooking the Delta. Site of the author's childhood home.

Grand Avenue
Residential and business avenue from Canal to Fifteenth Street and beyond.

Greenwood Leflore
Half French, half Indian early citizen who once owned the land on which much of Yazoo City now stands. Leflore was an important mediator between white settlers and Native Americans, including the Choctaws, Chickasaws, and Yazoos. Leflore County and the city of Greenwood are named for this statesman.

Glenwood Cemetery
Name of Yazoo City's most prominent cemetery where Revolutionary War veterans are buried. Site of "The Witch's Grave" made popular by Willie Morris. Located at the north end of Canal Street.

Holly Bluff
Community west of Yazoo City. Although much smaller, Holly Bluff High School enjoyed beating its arch rival,

Yazoo City High School, especially in basketball.

Jones, Casey
Legendary railroad engineer who died in a famous train crash in 1900 near Vaughan, in Yazoo County. A song and television series immortalized Jones' locomotive, "The Cannonball Express". The Casey Jones Museum is located at Vaughan.

Jonestown
Name of community across the Yazoo River from Yazoo City. The meandering river forms Jonestown Island.

Kudzu
Name of a parasitic vine planted to prevent soil erosion, and now occupies approximately 7,000,000 acres in the South.

Little Yazoo
Name of a small community located on Highway 49 ten miles south of Yazoo City.

Main Street
Yazoo City's central business district.

Main Street Elementary School
Early school building located on The Triangle where Main, Canal and Washington streets intersect.
In the 1950s, it was used as an elementary school.

Mingo Chito
Name of senior chief of the Yazoo tribe. Also name of the Yazoo City High School annual yearbook.

"Miss Firecracker"
Movie filmed in 1989 and based in Yazoo City. Performers

included Holly Hunter, Mary Steenbergen and Tim Robbins.

Mississippi Chemical Corporation
Founded in 1948 as the nation's largest farmer owned fertilizer corporative, MCC became the largest employer in the community.

Morris, Willie (1935-1999)
Born in Jackson, Willie Morris' family soon moved to Yazoo City. He excelled in writing and journalism. He became the youngest editor of Harper's Magazine, wrote many award winning books, and became the William Faulkner Professor at the University of Mississippi.

"My Dog Skip"
Book made into a movie in 2000 based on Willie Morris' childhood pet, Skip. Performers included Kevin Bacon, Frankie Muniz and Diane Lane.

Night Train
Rock and roll song and name of a popular teen rock and roll radio program on WAZF during the 1960s.

"O Brother, Where Art Thou"
Popular movie filmed in 2000 and based upon the area around Yazoo City. Performers included George Clooney, Holly Hunter, and John Goodman.

Oil City
Community near Tinsley in southeastern Yazoo County. Site of a brief oil boom in 1939.

"Old Yazoo"
Hit song written by Andy Razaf (author of "Ain't Misbehavin'" and "Honeysuckle Rose") and Fats Waller, in

1932 and recorded by the Boswell Sisters.

Panther Swamp National Wildlife Refuge
Site in eastern Yazoo County of a 36,000-acre protected habitat that contains one of the few remaining large tracts of mature bottomland hardwoods in the Mississippi delta.

Ricks Memorial Library
Name of the community library built by the B. S. Ricks family, and opened to the public in 1901. The library is one of the few buildings that escaped the fire of 1904. It is located on The Triangle near Main Street School.

Ricks Park
Formal name for a circular park on Grand Avenue popularly called Goose Egg Park.

Rolling Fork
Community west of Yazoo City in Sharkey County. Rolling Fork High was an arch rival of Yazoo City High when both schools were members of the Delta Valley Conference.

Satartia
Early community in Southwest Yazoo County. Once had a small high school that played against Yazoo City High, and often beat the larger school in basketball.

Shipyard, Confederate
A Confederate shipyard operated briefly during the Civil War at the top of Broadway hill. Ships were rolled down Broadway with logs and launched into the Yazoo River. Union forces burned the shipyard. Legend holds that the shipyard sawdust smoldered for a century, despite many attempts to extinguish it.

Southern Bag Corporation
Major employer, manufacturer of paper bags for many national vendors.

"Talk of the Town"
Name of a popular weeknight radio program that reported social news during the 1960s.

Teen Center
Sometimes call "The Hut," the Teen Center was a community youth activities center on Jackson Avenue.

Tinsley
Community in southeast Yazoo County near Oil City. Site of a brief oil boom.

Triangle, The
Cultural center bordered by the triangular intersections of Main Street, Washington Avenue, and Powell Street. Home to Ricks Memorial Library, Main Street School, and a Civil War statue.

Vaughan
Community on the eastern edge of Yazoo County north of Canton. Site of the famous crash of Casey Jones' Cannonball Express in 1900. Casey Jones Museum is located in Vaughan.

WAZF
Call letters for Yazoo City's popular radio station, 1230 on the AM dial. The station ceased operations in the 1980s.

Witch, Yazoo
Legendary woman who was suspected of being a murderess and witch. She threatened to come back from the grave

twenty years after her death in 1884 and burn down the town. Yazoo City almost burned completely to the ground in1904. Willie Morris chronicled the story in his book, "The Good Old Boy and The Witch of Yazoo".

Witch's Grave
Famous grave of "The Yazoo Witch" located in Glenwood Cemetery.

Wolf Lake
Popular fishing and boating lake west of Yazoo City.

Yazoo
The name probably means "death" or "river of death".

"Yazoo, Yazoo"
High School song composed by band director, Stanley Beers.

Yazoo City High School
School for grades nine through twelve located at the intersection of Canal and College. Grand Avenue begins at the intersection of Canal and College. Today, a larger, modern structure houses Yazoo City High.

Yazoo City Junior High
School for seventh and eighth grades located on Webster Avenue.

Yazoo County
Name of Mississippi's largest county (920 square miles).

Yazoo Indians
Name attributed to a fierce, but small nation of Native Americans, now extinct.

Yazoo Land Fraud
Name given to a Georgia based land fraud in 1795.

Yazoo River
Formed by the confluence of the Yalobusha and Tallahatchie Rivers, the Yazoo River is one of the major tributaries of the Mississippi River.

Yazooan
Name of a citizen or resident of Yazoo City or County.

Yazooan, The
Formerly "The Flashlight," the name given to the Yazoo City High School newspaper.

Ziglar, Zig
Born in Alabama, Zig Ziglar's family moved to Yazoo City where he grew up. Zig Ziglar is an internationally known motivational speaker, and calls Yazoo City home.

Printed in the United States
36003LVS00002B/133-201

9 781594 678011